SIMON B. RHYMIN'

SIMON B. RHYMIN'

BY **DWAYNE REED**

WITH **ELLIEN HOLI**

iLLUSTRATED BY
ROBERT PAUL JR.

LITTLE, BROWN AND COMPANY
New York Boston

MAY 1 1 2021

Copyright © 2021 by Dwayne Reed
Illustrations copyright © 2021 by Robert Paul Jr.

Cover art copyright © 2021 by Robert Paul Jr. Cover design by Jenny
Kimura. Cover copyright © 2021 by Hachette Book Group, Inc.

Little, Brown and Company
Hachette Book Group
1290 Avenue of the Americas, New York, NY 10104
Visit us at LBYR.com

First Edition: March 2021

Little, Brown and Company is a division of Hachette Book Group,
Inc. The Little, Brown name and logo are trademarks of Hachette
Book Group, Inc.

The publisher is not responsible for websites (or their content) that
are not owned by the publisher.

Library of Congress Cataloging-in-Publication Data
Names: Reed, Dwayne, author. | Holi, Ellien, author. |
Paul, Robert, Jr., illustrator.
Title: Simon B. Rhymin' / by Dwayne Reed with Ellien Holi ;
illustrated by Robert Paul Jr.
Description: First edition. | New York : Little, Brown and Company,
2021. | Audience: Ages 8–12 . | Summary: Chicago fifth-grader
Simon, an aspiring rapper who lacks self-confidence, uses his rhymes
to help bring his community together.
Identifiers: LCCN 2020039930 | ISBN 9780316538978 (hardcover) |
ISBN 9780316538947 (ebook) | ISBN 9780316538954 (ebook other)
Subjects: CYAC: Rap (Music)—Fiction. | Self-confidence—Fiction. |
African Americans—Fiction. | Chicago (Ill.)—Fiction.
Classification: LCC PZ7.1.R4278 Si 2021 | DDC [Fic]—dc23
LC record available at https://lccn.loc.gov/2020039930

ISBNs: 978-0-316-53897-8 (hardcover),
978-0-316-53894-7 (ebook)

Printed in the United States of America

LSC-C

Printing 1, 2020

MOMS, THANK YOU FOR TAKING
US TO ALL OF THOSE LIBRARIES AND
BOOKSTORES. THIS IS FOR YOU.
LOVE, MOOKIE

SUNDAY

CHAPTER 1

IT'S SIMON BARNES HERE. BUT EVERY--
body calls me the Notorious D.O.G., because I
might be little but I've got a loud bark. Okay, not
true. No one calls me the Notorious D.O.G. *yet*. But
they might one day when I'm a famous Chicago rapper like Kanye West or Chance the Rapper. Everybody from the Chi knows about them. For now, I'm
stuck with the nickname Rhymin' Simon, which my
brother DeShawn gave me when I was five because
I learned to rhyme and went kind of crazy with it.
Not too long after, I did my first remix to the itsy
bitsy spider song and my rhymes were extra basic.

THE ITSY BITSY SPIDER WAS LITTLE LIKE ME,

BUT HE COULD MAKE A WEB AS BIG AS

A TREE,

CLIMB TO THE TOP AND BE SO FREE,

 CUZ THE ITSY BITSY SPIDER WAS LITTLE

LIKE ME!

Those rhymes were cool back then, but, uh, I'm ready for something a little more tough, especially now that I'm eleven. The Notorious D.O.G. is something I'm trying out. It feels more like the *older* me.

I spent the whole weekend getting ready for fifth grade at Booker T. Washington Elementary School, where, this year, my class will be the oldest in the whole school. The first day is tomorrow, and I don't really feel ready for all this. On TV commercials, they show kids cheesin' real hard, happy to buy school supplies and new pairs of jeans. But don't they know that school means sitting still for hours and hours while the teacher is just talking at you about boring stuff, saying goodbye to playing Fortnite, and having to give up watching weird videos on YouTube? Goodbye to heating up pizza rolls whenever I feel like it and getting blue snow cones with DeShawn from the neighborhood ice cream truck, when he feels like splitting his time between me and his high school homies.

My mom is trying to give me a pep talk while we shop for some new clothes at Target. I usually wear hand-me-downs from my three older brothers, but my dad says *Every rising middle schooler deserves some fresh threads for school.* So, while I'm in a tiny red changing room putting on pairs of cargo pants among my big ol' pile of graphic tees and joggers, Mom tries to boost me up with her mom-knows-best motivational speech.

"C'mon, Simon. This year is gonna be *everything.* All your brothers had a ball in fifth grade. For real. Remember when Markus won that Invention Convention? He was so excited! Plus, you're gonna be the oldest kids in the school. Everybody will be looking up to you now!" Mom's voice sails over the tall fitting room door while other parents help their kids pull together outfits they won't have to fight about.

"Yeah, but I'll still be the shortest, Ma," I grumble, noticing that the pants she picked out for me have about four extra inches of fabric bunched up at the bottom.

"Short is a mind-set, Simon. To me, you're a million feet tall."

TALL?
NAH.
ME, I'M JUST SMALL.
COULD SHORT LITTLE SIMON
EVER SHINE LIKE A DIAMOND?
MY MOM THINKS SO,
BUT ME, I THINK NO.
HOPEFULLY, I CAN GROW,
HOPEFULLY, I CAN GROW.

"Stop letting those fools test you," she says, doing her best to put extra bass in her voice. I can't help but laugh to myself.

I look in the mirror and think my favorite vintage Chicago Bulls T-shirt doesn't look half bad with the rolled-up cargos and new Nike Air Maxes we bought yesterday. Not all the way Notorious, but hey, it's a start. I know they'll see me in this.

I LOOK INTO THE MIRROR, AND ALL I SEE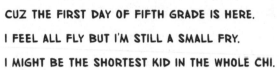
    IS FEAR,
CUZ THE FIRST DAY OF FIFTH GRADE IS HERE.
I FEEL ALL FLY BUT I'M STILL A SMALL FRY.
I MIGHT BE THE SHORTEST KID IN THE WHOLE CHI.

NERVOUS, BUT EXCITED, TO SEE OLD FRIENDS,
TO LAUGH, AND PLAY, AND LEARN AGAIN.
GOT MY SUPPLIES AND I'M READY TO GO,
CUZ TOMORROW, IT'S ON, AND THAT'S FA SHO'.

MAYBE I'LL GROW, OR JUST STAY THE SAME,
DOESN'T MATTER, THIS YEAR, THEY GON' SAY
    MY NAME.
PEOPLE GONNA KNOW ABOUT WEE OLD ME,
NOT SIMON, BUT NOTORIOUS D.O.G.!
WOOF! WOOF!

On our way home from Target, we run into my best friend Maria Rivera and her grandma, Ms. Estelle, in the parking lot. I don't think Estelle is her last name, but that's what everybody be callin' her. Maria yells my name too loud, surprising me, just as Mom and I finish throwing all my bags into the trunk. I jump, but only a little, cuz *Notorious D.O.G.* ain't never scared! I've been friends with Maria since the first grade. Sometimes we call her Ri-Ri because Rihanna is her favorite celebrity. My brothers call her Big Ol' Mouth because we always know what she's thinking about and nobody ever has more questions than her. But I like that she always knows what's going on, even when I don't.

MARIA, MARIA,
THAT'S MY AMIGA,
EVERY SINGLE TIME,
SHE'LL SAY WHAT'S ON HER MIND,
CONFIDENT AND KIND,
A GREAT FRIEND OF MINE,
MARIA, MARIA!

"Oh em GEEEE, SIMON! You ready for tomorrow? I heard our new teacher is really hard. Not strict like Mrs. Wright, but hard, like gives *real* work and actually makes us do it! Camille said she had a big project to do in the very first week of school last year," Maria says, pushing up her pink-rimmed glasses, squirming and waving her hands around in the air. I know it's a new pair cuz I've never seen these ones before, but they're too big just like all her other ones. None of her glasses ever fit enough to stay on her face. She's talking about school the same way she talks about everything else she's too hype about—as if she was telling me about some new sneakers or something. I wish that's what she really was telling me about. Camille is Maria's older sister, who's in middle school now and the source of a lot of Maria's info. I'm still not convinced that means we should believe her.

"Maria, ay Dios mío! Don't bother Simon with your silly gossip, now," Ms. Estelle says, dragging Maria toward the Target entrance. Maria has lived down the street from us since before I knew her, so we're always running into each other when she's out with her grandma shopping. "Just look at him. He looks like he's seen a fantasma from new school years past," she jokes, laughing at my blank face.

"Simon don't look like he's seen a ghost, 'Buela! That's just his face sometimes. He's probably just constipated," Maria says, flashing me an annoying smile while jabbing me in the shoulder. Instead of being quiet like most people, Maria makes up embarrassing stories about people to make herself laugh. She knows it's okay to do it to me but she'd never let somebody else embarrass me like that. "I'm not bothering him. We been talking about it *all* summer. Right, Simon? It's called the Freedom of Information Act, 'Buela. I make sure he knows what's up." Maria rolls her eyes at her grandma and waves a quick goodbye to me and Mom. I watch Ms. Estelle go off on her in Spanish while she skips toward the door like she's never seen a cloud in the sky.

As Mom and I get out of the car to walk toward our apartment building after unloading all my new school clothes, I can feel the butterflies floatin' around all crazy in my stomach. I'm not ready for us to be doin' nothin' too major in the first week of school. What if we have to get up in front of everybody?! Even though I can rap all I want at home, I just know I can't do anything like that in front of a whole classroom full of other kids. They all gon' be lookin' at me weird. Last time I tried to talk to a whole bunch of people, the room got spinny, my hands got sweaty, and I felt like I was gon' blow chunks all over the place! I guess even the Notorious D.O.G. can get the back-to-school, Sunday night blues.

MONDAY

CHAPTER 2

IF THE WEST SIDE HAD A HELICOPTER that could take people in the air to look down on different neighborhoods, Creighton Park probably would look like a big ol' rectangle with a whole lot going on inside. Like a shoe box with a bunch of toy cars, LEGOs, and pieces of broccoli in a little corner of it. And nobody really likes broccoli, so you wouldn't see any people in that part. I haven't left Creighton Park much since I was a little kid, and there's marks on the walls in our house to prove it. But that's okay because it feels like a whole world here.

Next to the big mirror that Dad put right by the front door, Moms (I call her that now sometimes. It'll stick one day!) has been marking up the wall to keep track of everybody's height. I once got in trouble when I drew a big S across my wall when I was learning how to write my name in preschool, but Moms says when she does it, it's different. *It helps you remember how far you've come*, she says. But I've been at the same mark on the wall for almost three years. On our way out the door for school, I take a quick look at myself to make sure, from the very first day, all the other kids see me as the new Notorious D.O.G. in my *new* Chicago Bulls T-shirt, black joggers with a white stripe down the side, and matching Air Maxes, scrubbed clean after I scuffed them a little bit on the way home last night.

HAIR LOOKS GOOD, CHECK!

NEW SHOES ON, FRESH!

BULLS T—SHIRT AND MY BLACK PANTS ON DECK!

FIRST—DAY SI, I'M FLY, THAT'S A BET!

THE D.O.G. IS SICK, SOMEBODY CALL A VET!

WOOF! WOOF!

"Hurry up, Simon. The way you movin' you'll be late for whatever fashion show you think you goin' to, baby." I give Moms a quick look out the corner of my eye. "Okay, big man. Let's go." She thinks this is a game.

We live in the Creighton Crest Apartments, and you can almost see my school from the sidewalk in front of our building. Me and Moms walk to the corner where the signs say LOCUST STREET and LOVING STREET, right before the corner store all the neighborhood kids go to for our candy, Flamin' Hots, and grape pop. Moms walks past it ahead of me so I won't ask her for nothin', like she's in a hurry. But I know me and Maria can probably get Ms. Estelle to stop there after school. Past Chicago Corner farther down Locust is Mr. Ray's Barbershop, where me, C.J., and Dad go to get fresh cuts every other Saturday. It's usually closed on Mondays, but today Mr. Ray is standing outside in front of the windows spray-painted WELCOME BACK TO SCHOOL, waving at all of us as we walk by even though we've seen him all summer. Mr. Ray seems just as excited as Maria for our first day.

"Mr. Barnes with the fresh cut! Watch out, now!" Old people always get weird about school and the first days of everything. Moms turns around to give me a look to make sure I'm not rude to him.

"Good morning, Mr. Ray," I say back through my teeth.

We pass the empty basketball court that will be full of high schoolers arguing and playing five-on-five when we get out later. Just then the sidewalk starts turning left into the school parking lot, packed with teachers' cars and teachers directing everybody in and out. Suddenly it feels like my heart is playing drums on the inside of my chest, getting faster and faster, louder and louder in my ears. Moms turns around and smiles. *Chill, Moms.*

Some kids call our school Booger T. Washington, but not me. I figure, since we spend five days a week in that place, might as well put a little respect on its name. Plus, I can't picture any famous rappers using the word *booger.*

MAYBE, JUST MAYBE, I'D SAY SNOT.

BUT BOOGER? OH <u>NAH!</u>

DEFINITELY <u>NOT!</u>

"Don't kiss me in front of everybody, okay?" I remind Moms just before we reach the steps to the front entrance. Even though that's what she always does when she drops me off anywhere, I don't need her blowing up my spot. It kinda makes me feel all fuzzy inside, but we can't be doing all of that now. This is fifth grade, feel me?

"I get it. Maybe I should pretend I'm not even your mom anymore," she says with a laugh as she gives my hand a quick squeeze, which still feels kind of good. She looks a little sad when she laughs, but I gotta be tough. Big new things are happening. "But all these other kids' moms probably still kiss them." I squeeze her hand back two times and hope she gets my message somewhere up there in Mom World.

Once we get to the playground outside of Booker T., Moms turns to me and gives me a weird

overhead high five that's probably just as embarrassing as a hug. "Have a good day, Simon. I luhh you."

Gah!

"Don't forget to use that voice today, big guy,"
she says before leaving.

Maria is already in the line for fifth graders and
saved me a spot. I slouch against the tall brick school
building looking down on me, keeping my eye out
for my other best friend, C.J., who's always late, even
on important days like the first day of school.

"Siiiiimon! Earth to Siiiiimon!" Maria always
says stuff like that to me when she wants my attention, whether it's about something important—
Chess Club got moved to room 302—or something
not-so-important—*That new Drake song is fire!
You heard it yet, Simon?*

"What?!"

"I was saying, do you have all your stuff ready?
I sharpened my pencils last night and labeled all
of my different-colored folders so I could be prepared. *By failing to prepare, you're preparing to fail.*
My tío has that written on a poster in his office,"
she explains in her deepest, most serious voice.

"Oh, and I did a bunch of multiplication flash cards last night before I went to bed, because Camille told me I'd better be ready for more math this year. What about you?" This is when Maria turns and looks me right in the eye, all up in my face like she, too, is one of our new teachers. She's big on eye contact and gets real serious when she asks her questions. She's already doing the most.

"Umm, yeah. Yup…," I say, trying to ignore the pit that's forming in my stomach. More math? I hate math. And flash cards? Who gets excited about more flash cards and memorizing number stuff?

MATH'S HARD! FLASH CARDS?

NO WAY, NO THANKS!

 ALL THOSE QUOTES AND STICKY NOTES—NOPE, NOPE, NOPE!

Camille is probably just trying to scare us like her and her friends always do. And Maria's love of fancy quotes and school supplies makes me feel kinda low. I guess I'm not really excited for school like she is.

I pull my new all-blue book bag tighter onto my back, squeezing the shoulder straps, and feel the gold Black Panther pin I attached to it press against the inside of my hand. It's already too heavy, filled with proof that Moms overdid it once again. I didn't do everything Maria did last night, but by the weight of this thing, I know *something* in there will work.

Just then, C.J. runs up, breathing extra hard and wiping sweat off his forehead. Of course he ran all the way here. We all look at one another and bust out laughing. C.J.—short for Cornelius Jeremiah— is always a hilarious dude to look at with his lop-sided T-shirt and shorts riding up his butt after an almost-late morning school hustle. His first-day look ain't no different than any other: This morning he's rockin' his favorite yellow Goku tee, his dad's hand-me-down dark red basketball shorts, and mismatched Steven Universe socks inside a pair of classic high-top Chucks that he probably won't ever stop wearing until they're so old his feet rip through the soles and his toes are barking through the front. He made sure to seal the look with his signature high-top fade and an extra-crispy side part right above his left eyebrow.

MY BIG HOMIE C.J., AS COOL AS IT GETS,

SO CONFIDENT, FROM HIS HAIR TO HIS 'FITS,

A HILARIOUS DUDE, FUNNY DOWN TO HIS BONES,

I'M GLAD HE'S MY FRIEND, CORNELIUS JONES.

"Whoo, I made it!" C.J. says, smiling and opening a medium-sized bag of Flamin' Hot Cheetos. I'm pretty sure he loves them just about as much as he loves anime, playing ball, and watching Saturday morning cartoons while FaceTiming us from the couch leaned over a bowl of Fruity-O's. He low-key probably loves eating Flamin' Hots just as much as he loves old-school Derrick Rose. So...that means, A LOT. He pulls out a handful and stuffs them in his mouth all at once. You'd think he didn't have breakfast like he does every morning with his little sister, but we know this is just Breakfast: Part Two. "Y'all know you want some. Corn and cheese

are breakfast foods, don't be lookin' at me all funny." We crack up at this speech we've heard a million times.

I've been friends with C.J. since I was really little, so we're basically cousins. That's how it is on the West Side—anybody that's not your cousin can still be your cousin if they've known your family long enough. It's weird, but it's a thing. I even call his mom Auntie Sharon. But that's also because I'd have big problems with my mom if I called a grown-up just by their first name. And I don't want those problems. C.J.'s tall and big, so people think he's tough. But the joke's on them, because he's kind of like a teddy bear, actually, and he loves watching Disney movies, on top of his regular cartoon faves, with his little sister. But I'm not snitchin' on him because I don't mind other kids thinking C.J. is a big, bad part of the Notorious D.O.G. squad. I want kids to think he's like my security or something—especially kids like Bobby Sanchez.

"Hey, Simon. Did you get *any* taller over the summer? They're probably gonna send you back to kindergarten for being so short, so I don't even know why you're in the fifth-grade line, bruh!" Bobby teases, jabbing his elbows into his friends' sides, egging them on to laugh. Bobby has walked up with his friends Justin Cook and Victor G., and they both look at me and laugh a little too hard along with their leader. All three of them are dressed like it's basketball season—Bobby in his usual extra-long white tee, some vintage-looking Pistons shorts, and what look like hand-me-down all-white Air Force 1s—even though all of them would be better talkin' stuff on the sidelines. They're the kind of kids who make a lot of noise wherever they go, even if they're not really saying anything anybody else wants to hear.

I try to think of something—anything!—to say back to Bobby, but the words just won't come out of my mouth.

SEE, I CAN'T STAND THIS STUFF,
BOBBY SANCHEZ ALWAYS MAKING THINGS
   TOUGH,
 PICKING ON ME CUZ I'M SMALLEST IN THE
   GROUP,
WISH I HAD THE GUTS TO STAND UP TO HIS
   CREW!
I'D SAY SOME OF THIS AND PROBABLY SOME OF
   THAT,
THEN EVERYONE WOULD LAUGH AT MY FUNNY
   CLAPBACKS.
BUT THAT AIN'T ME, I'M THE NICE ONE, SEE?
SMALL GUY, BIG HEART, NOTORIOUS D.O.G.

Briiiiing! Briiing!
Now here's the bell. Oh, class. School. Right.

CHAPTER 3

WELCOME, SCHOLARS!

These words are written across the whiteboard in big, bold letters. *Scholars?* Most teachers at Booker T. call us plain ol' students. Ms. Berry, the principal, sometimes tries out *citizens of the school community,* and we once had a really old substitute teacher who kept calling us *pupils* (what IS that, though?), but no one has used the word *scholars.* This guy already seems weird, but when we walk in he shakes all of our hands and looks us in the eyes. He seems like he's actually hype to see us. Weirder. But his smile makes me feel kind of okay. A teacher that looks as young as he does who calls us schol-ars wouldn't pull some big project business on the first week. Right?

"Good morning, 5-B!" the guy, our teacher, Mr. James, says with a huge grin on his face. Mr. James looks way younger than Dad and only a lit-tle bit older than my big brothers—so, young for a teacher—and is wearing a bright red bow tie *and* tennis shoes. Bold move. Some of the other kids look confused, piling into our new classroom with desks that don't have names stuck to them in bright colored letters like every other year. I grab the desk one row behind Maria, who sits in the front, as always. From behind her big curly hair that Ms. Estelle pulled into a big puff at the top, I watch Mr. James walk around the room, waiting for us to say something back.

"Morning," a few of my classmates barely whis-per, like they're still half asleep and mostly scared. Mr. James smiles all by himself, looking like he thinks it's funny.

"Good morning, Mr. James!" Maria says in her loudest, perkiest voice. She can't help herself.

It almost looks like she's gonna jump out of her seat.

"Maria, Camille Rivera's little sister! I'm expecting excellent work from you. Your sister set the bar high." Maria smiles at the compliment. She's proud of her hermana—and anything that'll save her a spot as the teacher's favorite, early. I'm cool with the distraction while I look around at the walls covered in pictures of little kids from other classes Mr. James had before us. I know they're his classes because he's in so many of them, leaned over desks, pointing to whiteboards, and high-fiving like it's the best day ever, dressed in a different-colored bow tie and matching sneakers like it's his own special uniform. The rest of the room looks like half a box of crayons exploded on the walls. The wall where we came in is a bright red just like Mr. James's tie, and the wall in the back is a dark yellow, Maria's favorite. The wall with all the windows is a dark green, which makes it look like it's blending in with the trees outside, and the wall behind Mr. James is a bright blue covered in random quotes. We all sit like rows of brown crayons in a box facing the front—following

Mr. James's every move, careful not to do anything to make him call our names. He walks to the middle of the floor where the big aisle he's made with the desks is and puts one of his sneakers up on a chair. The biggest of the blue wall quotes is taped above his head: I KNOW I CAN.

"Everyone, take a look at the whiteboard and repeat after me: *I'm more than a student, I'm a scholar!*" Mr. James excitedly raises his hands up in the air, trying to get a bunch of us to follow along. Nobody moves at first just in case it's some type of fifth-grade trick our big brothers and sisters ain't tell us about. Plus, it's too early for this!

"I'm more than a student, I'm a scholar," Maria and about two other kids say, Maria's words sounding like a nursery rhyme. She's ruining it for the rest of us. Mr. James's corny smile stays the same for a second and then gets bigger. Another joke none of us can hear. It almost seems like he enjoys the challenge.

"C'mon now. Y'all gon' have to do better than that! Again, repeat after me: *I'm more than a student, I'm a scholar!*" This time, instead of just raising his hands, Mr. James lunges up on top of his desk, feet almost dancing between work sheets, pens, and different-colored markers. My guy is up in front of the class, hopping around on a table, waving his hands all over the place like he's at a concert! "I'm more than a student, I'm a scholar! AYE! I'm more than a student, I'm a scholar! AYE!" When he hops back off his desk and bounces down the aisles to the rhythm, a few kids next to me start repeating his words while looking around at one another to see if we're really doing this.

"Yo, I'm more than a student, I'm a scholar!" Justin Cook, Bobby Sanchez's wingman, calls out from the back of the room, making fun of Mr. James. But when everybody hears him, the whole class cashes in on the chance to get loud, leaning, rocking, and snapping like it's the hook of one of our favorite rap songs.

I'M MORE THAN A STUDENT, I'M A SCHOLAR, AYE!

I'M MORE THAN A STUDENT, I'M A SCHOLAR, AYE!

I'M MORE THAN A STUDENT, I'M A SCHOLAR, AYE!

"I'm a school-er!" This is Lil Kenny, a kid who always seems like he lives in his own world. Before I can stop myself, I'm chanting with the class, too.

"Okay, okay." Mr. James laughs, lowering his hands from the sky to get the class to calm down and get back in our seats. Lil Kenny follows his lead and comes all the way down from standing on top of his desk, too, looking glad that he's not in trouble for getting that reckless on the first day. Mr. James moves into the new-school-year speech that all teachers give and I think the chanting is over, but all of a sudden...

GOOD MORNING TO MY SCHOLARS WHO ARE IN
    FIFTH GRADE,
BET YOU NEVER THOUGHT YOU'D HEAR A
    TEACHER SPIT THIS WAY.
SEE, MY NAME'S MR. JAMES, AND THE REASON I
    CAME
WAS TO TEACH YOUNG PEOPLE, WHILE KEEPIN' IT
    FLAME.

I WAS RAISED BY MY MAMA, WHO WAS BLACK
    AND STRONG,
HAD A BROTHER AND A SISTER WHO WOULD TAG
    ALONG,
GOT MY HIGH SCHOOL DIPLOMA, THEN MY
    COLLEGE DEGREE,
AND THEN I MOVED BACK TO THE CITY THAT
    MADE ME.

THAT'S THE CHI—AND YOU KNOW I REP OUT WEST.
I BECAME A TEACHER SO THAT I COULD HELP
    THE BEST.
ALL THESE KIDS RIGHT HERE, GONNA CHANGE
    THE WORLD.
I'M EXCITED TO LEARN FROM YOU BOYS AND GIRLS.

♪ SO THIS YEAR IS QUITE DIFFERENT, IT'S FINNA
BE HYPE.

WE GON' LEARN A LOT TOGETHER IN THIS
CLASSROOM, AIGHT?

IT'S GON' ALL BE LOVE, HARD WORK, AND GRACE.

I'M SO HAPPY THAT WE'RE HERE TOGETHER IN ♪
THIS PLACE.

Welcome to class!

5-B explodes. Kids clap, stomp, and scream *Aaaaaye* while some run up to Mr. James to dap him up. Lil Kenny leaps out of his chair and does a lap around the whole classroom like an old lady at church who just caught the Holy Ghost. Even Bobby and his minions are impressed. "OKAY! OH-KAY!" screams Victor, shaking his head like Mr. James just got his approval. "You lit, Mr. James! Go on 'head!" Lil Kenny takes a second lap as Maria turns to me with eyes bulging so big they look like they're gonna pop out of her head.

SI-MON, she mouths. *OH EM GEEE*, she mouths again, squeezing her eyes tight just before jumping out of her seat to clap. Notorious D.O.G.

can't get too hype on the first day, but WOW! I never would have guessed that my fifth-grade teacher would also be a rapper. And he's actually kinda good! Man, Mr. James and the Notorious D.O.G. might have to do a music collab in the future. But that's only if I ever get the confidence to show off my skills in front of *real* people—well, people other than just my parents and brothers.

Mr. James drops his imaginary microphone so he can then drop the first bomb on us. "We'll be getting right down to business starting today so you all can show me what you're working with." This is when he picks up the pile of papers he was standing over on his desk just a few minutes ago and puts a stack on one desk at the end of each row. "One of the best ways to get to know somebody is to find out what they really care about," he says as we all pass the stacks of mysterious paper down the rows. Not gonna lie. Mr. James sounds just as cloudy as the teacher off the *Peanuts* cartoons when he says "down to business." He might as well have been saying *Blah blah blahddy blah bloop.* Every time a teacher says *business* they mean *work*, and up until right now I'd forgotten all about that.

Maria turns in her chair and passes the stack to me with the most annoying smile on her face. "SEEEEE? Camille was right!" She beams, pointing her finger to the words that read *ORAL PRESEN-TATION* and *DUE BY ALPHABETICAL ORDER.* The first-week project Maria's big sister was talking about is a BIG OL' ORAL PRESENTATION. And now I'm *big* mad. And because my last name starts with *B*, that can only mean one very scary thing. I almost forget to pass the rest of the copies behind me until a paper ball slaps the back of my head. I turn just in time to see Bobby grinning to himself.

"I know what y'all are thinking." *Nah, cuz if you knew, you wouldn't do this to me, Mr. James*, I almost say aloud. "Presentation? Noooooo!" I'd laugh at Mr. James making fun of how we all feel, but my armpits are already dripping. "Due next week? Heeeeelp!" He keeps on while my eyeballs try to read the work sheet, but I can't get past the due date and the fact that I—

"But check this out: It can be on whatever you want! What's something that you care about A LOT that you want others to care about, too?"

"FORTNITE!"

"CHIPS!"

"PLAYING BALL WITH MY COUSINS!"

"WHEN MY MAMA BE TAKIN' ME SHOPPIN' AT THE MALL! We need to do that every day!" The whole class explodes again while Mr. James stands in the front smiling, shaking his head into his hand. "For real, Mr. James. It's important! She always talkin' about how we ain't got no money!" Mr. James's head pops up like Lil Kenny's screaming out his mom's business is the smartest thing he's ever heard.

"That's it, Kenny. Maybe one thing you care about that you could do your presentation on is money. Going to the mall every day might be a little unrealistic," Mr. James says, walking down the aisle and stopping in front of Kenny's desk. "But maybe...you can talk about one of the reasons why parents might not be able to take us to the mall as much as we might want. Let's think a little deeper past video games, food, playing, and shopping, y'all. What are some things that make it hard for you to enjoy these things in your community? Think of something timely—meaning something important going on right now—that is making it hard for a lot of people to enjoy things they like or need." Now I know Mr. James be on some other stuff. What's deeper than food and Fortnite? Nothing could keep me from either...could it? "While you all think about that, let's go over the presentation order so everybody's clear on when to be ready."

FIFTH GRADE IS CRAZY, IT'S STARTING WITH A
    TWIST—
A YOUNG, RAPPING TEACHER, HOW COOL IS THIS?
HE ROCKS BOW TIES AND TENNIS SHOES, THAT'S
    FLY.
I MEAN, HE'S KINDA CORNY, BUT HE'S STILL A
    COOL GUY.

THIS PRESENTATION, THOUGH? FOR ME, THAT'S
    A NO!
I'M NOT FEELIN' IT, LIKE IT'S TWO FEET OF SNOW,
LIKE I'M WAITIN' IN A LONG LINE AT THE
    GROCERY STO'.
I LIKED HOMIE'S FLOW, BUT THIS MESS GOTTA
    GO!

Most of us have been at Booker T. since kinder-garten. I got here in the middle of first grade, but that makes me an old head, too, by now. It's Mr. James that's kinda new...to us, at least. I already know my life is over once I see we have to go in alphabetical order. I've been called on first for almost everything since I was five. Never for anything this big, though. Under my desk I cross my fingers super hard that somebody new has a last name that starts with A. After I look behind me where Bobby and Friends sit leaned up against the yellow wall, to my right where the red wall probably matches my cheeks, and to my left where rows of kids I know sit under the windows surrounded by green, my stomach starts feeling as queasy as the things that color made me think of. Boogers...puke...the fart steam you see coming up when somebody lets out a funky one in cartoons...

"Up first, next Monday, Simon Barnes." Fingers crossed never works!

"That's my friend, Mr. James! That's my friend!" Maria is more excited than I could ever be. So excited, I want to beg Mr. James to let us switch places. But Maria's last name is too far down the alphabet, and right then my voice crawls down into my stomach to hide. For a second, Mr. James looks me in the eye before he continues reading out the rest of the names. Even though I dreamed of being up on a stage making the crowd go crazy at home, I squirm in my seat at the thought of it now. Being the youngest of four brothers and the shortest kid in every grade so far makes me used to never being seen. Not in a cool way, at least.

CHAPTER 4

"C.J., I'M OVER IT. I CAN'T DO IT." BY THE time we both get to the cafeteria, half of the tables are full and I find C.J. near the front of the line, where he lets me squeeze in front of him as always. We stop every few steps to have one of the lunch workers drop each thing on our trays, even though we won't eat half of it. Last year C.J. always tried to get Ms. Kathy to give him double of whatever it was and she always shooed him away like a fly, telling him he needed to slow down and be grateful. C.J. stops in front of her station bouncing his eyebrows, flashing all his teeth, and she drops something extra on his tray. A fifth-grade flex.

"Whatchu talkin' 'bout, Simon? We ain't even ate yet, man." C.J. makes sure to dap Ms. Kathy up in the air before we slide our trays down to the end of the lunch counter. I size up Booker T.'s boxy cafeteria that also gets used as the auditorium on holidays. Maria always calls it a big ol' bowl of Fruity-O's cuz the walls look like milk and each table is round and a different color. I ask her to explain the old signs on the walls about boring nutrition and all the brown kids sitting at the tables. *All cereal boxes have a bunch of words on them, duh. And sometimes I mix Reese's Puffs into my Fruity-O's, Simon. It still tastes good.*

C.J. walks off toward all the tables like he already knows where to sit. Because he does. I guess going to the same school for five years does that. It's the same ol' place and he's headed to our spot at the center table where it's still empty, just waiting for our squad to fill it up.

We sit down on the hard plastic seats that stick out and float from under the table like something out of the future even though they're old and rag-gedy. We both know not to sit on the busted yellow seat that spins. We know it's gonna be broken forever. Sitting down while balancing trays of popcorn chicken, some weird-looking vegetable, small cups of syrupy fruit, and cartons of chocolate milk, me and C.J. sit across from each other. Neither of us eats all that stuff, but we have favorites. We both keep the popcorn chicken, but Maria gets the fruit cups, C.J. gets our chocolate milk, and we find Lil Kenny and give him the vegetables. He's the only kid who doesn't care that he can't tell what it is and will eat pretty much anything. I put my milk carton on a seat next to me to save it for Maria.

"I'm not talking about the food, C.J."

"What else is there to talk about right now, *Notorious C.A.T.*? It's lunchtime." C.J. is arranging his extra nuggets on the tray to make enough space for all the extra sauces he's about to mix together next to them. He swears BBQ and may-onnaise hits different. Me and Maria usually try not to look.

"Notorious D.O.G.," I say with a groan. This

nickname is gon' take some work. If people are gonna see the new, bigger me, it has to catch on with my friends first.

"Right. Anyway, Simon, what you mad at, then?"

"Okay, so our new teacher, Mr. James, jumps up on his desk and starts rappin' about—"

"Wait, WHAT?"

"He jumps on the desk and starts rappin' about his mama, his high school diploma, and working hard and then he—" C.J. puts both of his arms out, signaling me to stop.

"BRUH! You got a teacher that be rappin' on his desk and you over it?!" C.J. pretends to scratch his head to show his confusion but avoids actually scratching his head so he doesn't mess with his fresh cut. He moves his hand to his chin and leans in. "I don't get it, Simon."

"I didn't finish! He tricked us, C.J.! After he got done he told us we gotta do an oral presentation. We gotta stand in front of everybody and talk... already!" I stand up in the middle of what I'm saying while trying to explain my problem to C.J., and just then I realize it, plopping back down on the bench feeling like a busted balloon again. "He just kept smiling about it."

"Sounds like you got the nice, fun teacher. My teacher, Mrs. Leary, is at least five hundred years old and told us we need to 'keep our nose to the grindstone,' whatever that means. She prolly hates rap." C.J. isn't even exaggerating. Me and Maria saw her bony, wrinkly hand reach out from behind her door like Jack Skellington out of *Nightmare Before Christmas*. We saw her shuffle to the door to welcome C.J. into her class right before we went into ours. There might have even been a cane, but we didn't stand there long enough to find out for sure. C.J. frowns, looking like he's imagining sticking his nose against some kind of rock for the whole year to help him make it to middle school.

"Maybe you're right," I say, dunking a stale piece of popcorn chicken into some barbecue sauce. I don't know why they call it popcorn chicken when it tastes nothing like popcorn. It's a big lie. Either way, it ain't got nothing on Dad's spicy chicken tenders, but BBQ sauce seems to make anything taste better.

YEAH, IT'S TRUE, BABY, YES IT'S TRUE, EVERYTHING TASTES BETTER WITH SOME BBQ!

"But what about the oral presentations he said we have to do? That don't sound fun to me at all!" Flashbacks come to me of hearing the words *presentation* and *alphabetical order* and *Monday*. Even my brain feels like it's covered in goose bumps. "We're supposed to get up in front of the whole class and talk about something that's 'timely.'"

"What's *timely* mean?" C.J. asks after taking a gulp of his first chocolate milk.

"It means something that's important in our world right now. Something that matters to kids here at Booker T. or to people in Creighton Park." Maria butts in to the conversation as she sits down, plunking her super SHE-roes lunch bag on the table. Me and C.J. stare into a big colorful picture of an older Black woman who looks like my granny Lucille, with a crispy Afro, circle-ly glasses, and a patchy sweater, on the side of the bag as Maria pulls it open to check out Ms. Estelle's leftovers that she packed for today. We already know the old lady on her bag's name is Octavia Butler because Maria wouldn't stop talking about her all summer when we were learning how to build electrified fences in Fortnite. *Octavia predicted this would happen in the future!* she would say. *Camille said that in Octavia's book everybody has gates around their houses because it's too dangerous to go outside!* I just thought it was cool that she had a name that sounded like one of the girls in our neighborhood.

"Like how Derrick Rose is the best basketball player ever, even though he's not playing for the Bulls anymore?" C.J. says, warming up to the idea but not really getting it. "That matters a lot! People need to know about his greatness! Vintage D-Rose!" Maria rolls her eyes while holding her hand out for our fruit cups.

"Umm...not exactly. More like, how to get healthier food into schools," Maria says, scrunching up her face at our half-eaten chicken nuggets, then pulling a plastic bowl of rice and beans out of her lunch box. "'Buela says the food here got too much salt in it."

"Salt makes everything taste better, though! That can't be timely. Salt's a good thing. I *looove* salt." C.J. licks all sides of a nugget, then dunks it in his cup of BBQ sauce before taking a bite. Me and Maria stare until he finally looks up and sees us fake-gagging at his nasty nugget eating.

"What?"

"Salt makes it take longer to grow molds on your nuggets!" Maria bites into a slice of plantain and continues. "So they could be old but you wouldn't even know it. Anyway, like I was saying, something like the environment or homelessness or crime." I don't get how she can be so happy worrying about the world's problems. But even worse: I don't get how either of us can do a whole project on one in front of everybody.

"So, when do these big talkie-talks start? Y'all probably have a bunch of time, right? Mrs. Leary ain't give us no real homework yet. She spent the whole class practicing our names and told us to write something in our journals about where our names came from," C.J. says, already packing up to hit the playground for recess with chocolate milk still drizzling down the side of his mouth. "All I gotta write on the paper is *My mama*. The end." I wish I had that assignment.

"Nope, they start next week!" Maria said. "And guess who got picked to go first? SIMON!"

CHAPTER 5

AT THE END OF THE DAY, MS. ESTELLE waits for me and Maria at the bottom of the front steps of Booker T. I've told my mom I'm old enough to do the four-block walk by myself, but the answer is always no. So Ms. Estelle usually walks me and Maria home and then I hang out with one of my brothers—usually Markus, who's in the seventh grade and thinks he's waaaay older than me—until Moms gets back from work at the hospital. When she gets home she makes me do homework at the kitchen counter while she takes a shower and figures out what her and Dad are gonna do about dinner.

I usually rush so I can play at least one game with Maria and C.J. online. *We have a system, Simon. Don't mess with our system*, Moms always says.

Before we even get to the end of the sidewalk by the school parking lot, Maria is busy going on and on to Ms. Estelle about every single thing that happened on our first day, but I don't really have much to say. Mr. James told us we needed to give a presentation on an issue that's important to us or to our community. And because I'm the most unlucky kid on the West Side of Chicago, I got picked to go first. How am I supposed to talk in front of the whole class next week?! How am I supposed to know enough about something to make sense of it in just a week? It seems impossible. It seems like the only person who knows how impossible it is, is me.

I'M STRESSIN', I'M STRESSIN',
AIN'T GOT NO DIRECTION!
DON'T ASK ME NO QUESTIONS,
 I WON'T TAKE SUGGESTIONS!
I FEEL LIKE A MESS,

AND MY BEST FRIEND IS MESSIN'
WITH ME, 'BOUT THIS LESSON.
I'M STRESSIN', I'M STRESSIN'.

"And guess what, Abuela? Mr. James is having everyone give a talk about big, important topics, and Simon gets to go first! Next Monday!" Maria says to Ms. Estelle, turning to smile at me. I look back at her, forcing a fake half smile so I won't have to say anything. I wish the smile could be real, and Maria probably knows it isn't.

I remember how we moved to Creighton Park right before winter break when I was seven, and Mr. Peterson, our first-grade teacher, gave me a part in the holiday play, even though I was too new to even know what was going on.

"I like your costume, Simon," Maria told me, appearing next to me out of nowhere during our dress rehearsal. Because she was little like me, it always felt like she was sneaking up on people. "I wish Mr. Peterson chose me to be a snowman," she went on, looking down at her sparkling legs and then her sparkling arms. She was a snowflake. There was nothing cool or fun about being picked to be a snowman in a winter play, because I just stood there saying nothing in a hat with a scarf around my neck and a fake carrot tied to my face. At least she could still use her legs. But Maria would smile at me from wherever she was onstage or clap the hardest from her seat in the auditorium when it was my turn to stand under the spotlight looking like what me and my brothers made when the snow got really heavy outside. It was easy to say yes when she asked me to be her friend because she acted like everything I did would be the best even though I never did anything that great. She thought it was cool that I could climb so easily through the tunnels at the playground when the other kids said I looked small enough to still be in preschool. The first day Bobby made fun of the size of my head in front of the whole class, she said I probably had five brains in my head instead of just one like everyone else. "Bobby has a coconut head, anyway," she told me at lunch. "'Buela says when you crack a coconut open, only water comes out. That's Bobby's head. He got a coconut head and no brain." I'd never seen a whole coconut before and when I thought about coconut I thought of the nasty little white pieces on top of one of the cakes my granny liked to make and only the old people liked to eat. Thinking of water exploding from the head of the meanest kid in school made me laugh until chocolate milk mixed with snot came squirting out of my nose Super Soaker–style. As annoying as she can be sometimes, she's always made me laugh at silly stuff like that.

"Muy exciting" is all Ms. Estelle has to say now. Maria would continue even if no one said anything to her ever.

"I'm already putting together a list of ideas and topics for my presentation. I bet Mr. James is gonna need to give me two times to share. Five minutes isn't enough, 'Buela!" Ms. Estelle continues looking in front of us, quietly smiling. A basketball hoop chain jingles to the right of us before a ball flies over the fence above our heads as we walk by Locust Court. A high schooler comes running out into the street after it and I look to see if Aaron, my oldest brother, is playing with his friends. I'd rather be playing than thinking about a project already.

An oral presentation is the perfect assignment for Maria, actually. She has feelings and thoughts about everything. I usually hang out with my brothers and pretend to start my homework when I get home from school until my parents get off work. C.J. does the same thing with his sister. Maria told me she usually helps Ms. Estelle chop onions, clean vegetables, or season meat before her parents get home from work. And after dinner, she sits with her watching the news. Maria can speak English better than Ms. Estelle and so Ms. Estelle sometimes needs Maria to tell her in Spanish what's being said. It sounds boring to me, but Maria always says it's cool that we can know what's going on everywhere in the world just by watching TV.

"What about you, Simon? What you gonna do?" Ms. Estelle squeezes my shoulder.

"Uh, that's top secret right now. I can't tell you that, Ms. E," I say, trying to cover up how clueless I feel. I don't feel like telling her the truth, which is that I don't have any ideas at all, and my armpits are sweating so bad I'm glad we're almost to my house so nobody but Markus will see the big wet stains on my new T-shirt.

UGH! I HATE THIS, I ABSOLUTELY HATE THIS!
WHY DO KIDS HAVE TO DO ORAL
    PRESENTATIONS?!
WHY CAN'T WE JUST WRITE ABOUT WHAT OUR
    NAME IS?
OR READ STORIES TALKIN' 'BOUT PEOPLE WHO
    ARE FAMOUS?

I MEAN, MR. JAMES IS COOL...I GUESS,
BUT THIS PROJECT IS LIKE...DUDE, WHAT THE
    HECK?!
AND I'M GOING FIRST! I SWEAR, IT'S THE WORST!
FIFTH GRADE IS ALREADY TOO MUCH WORK!

I DON'T HAVE ANY IDEA WHAT TO SAY.
MAYBE I SHOULD TALK ABOUT THE FIRST
    SCHOOL DAY?
AND HOW IT'S PLAIN WRONG TO MAKE KIDS DO
    THIS!
YUP, THAT'S MY TOPIC, THAT'S WHAT I'LL PICK!
WOOF! WOOF!

As we get closer to the corner just before Loving Street, Maria looks at me and I know we need to get Ms. Estelle to reward us for a great first day. It wasn't great for me, but neither of us got sent to the principal's office, and we know that will convince Ms. Estelle to give us money for snacks even if it wouldn't work on my mom.

"'Buela, Mr. James even knew I was Camille's sister and he said he expects great things from me," Maria says with her eyes all big.

"Ay Dios mío. You babies are so smart."

"'Buela."

"Yes, baby?"

"Can we—"

"I knew you wanted the candies. Simon, just don't tell your madre, okay?" Ms. Estelle hands us both a dollar and we run into Chicago Corner. With a dollar we each can get a bag of chips and some Frooties. In minutes we're both back out on the sidewalk, stuffing our brown paper bags deep into our backpacks with the door jingling behind us.

We turn onto Loving Street and walk down the long pathway up to Creighton Crest Apartments, where I see Sunny pushing a broom up and down the sidewalk. The sidewalk is mostly clean from him sweeping in front of our building just a few days ago, but he never lets all the empty candy wrappers and random pop bottles pile up in our neighborhood. Sunny is somebody who's like my grandpa that I've seen around our neighborhood since we moved here, but I don't really know where he lives. All I know is that he's usually sweeping up the sidewalks and that he's always nice to me and my brothers.

"Hey-o, Rhymin' Simon and Miss Maria! Back to school? Hitting the books?" Sunny says to us with a pile of empty chip bags and cans in front of him. I don't know if it was Dad or Moms who snitched about DeShawn naming me that because I rap, but it stuck and it's all he's called me ever since. He looks funny standing in front of us in clothes that look like they belong to somebody much bigger than he is. Today he wears a stretched-out-looking blue polo shirt with a tag on his chest that says MECHANIC on it with a little bit of his gray-haired chest poking out where buttons used to be.

His jeans seem kind of new, but he keeps having to pull them up every few steps. He pushes random candy wrappers into the trash pile with his once-white Air Force 1s that never had shoelaces but, somehow, he keeps them on. I think he's had the same ones the whole time I've known him.

"Hi, Sunny," Maria and I say at the same time.

"Let's get you home, Simon," Ms. Estelle says, suddenly picking up speed toward my building. We aren't far and it's gonna be a long time before it gets dark out, but it seems like the minute Ms. Estelle sees Sunny trying to talk to us, we need to move faster. Ms. Estelle rushes to the gate at the front of my apartment building, barely letting me and Maria say too much more. I've never seen Ms. Estelle rush anywhere, but it seems like Sunny makes her a little nervous.

As I open the gate, I hear Sunny singing a song to himself while he sweeps.

Grab your coat, grab your hat.

Sweep, sweep.

Don't you worry 'bout this and that.

Sweep, sweep, sweep.

Move your feet, on the sunny side of the street.

Sunny almost sounds like somebody else's voice is coming out of his body. How he sings is better than most of the old folks who be singin' in the choir at church on Sunday mornings. Compared to Sunny's smooth hums, they sound like tires screeching against the street right before an accident. I don't understand how he can sing like that, but it doesn't seem like he has anywhere to perform for real.

Ms. Estelle carefully locks the gate behind me while she watches me walk up the stairs to our apartment, even though the Notorious D.O.G. don't need anybody watching his every move. Before I go inside, I see her look over her shoulder at Sunny as he keeps singing some song that sounds like it was written one thousand years ago but is still his favorite. He stops sweeping and looks up at me from the street while he weaves my name into the lyrics and bows.

Told Rhymin' Simon, don't you worry 'bout this and that!

I clap inside.

CHAPTER 6

"I JUST DON'T UNDERSTAND HOW YOU CAN play yourself like that. We all know they fake!" Aaron hovers above the three of us with his hands raised in the air the way he does whenever an argument gets serious.

"Not everybody. If you get them from the right store, it's like getting the real thing without having to spend all your allowance money." Markus tries to convince him.

"We don't get no allowance money, fool," DeShawn points out. True.

"Exactly. If you already broke, why spend your

little money on some busted sneakers that ain't even the real thing? You just asking for somebody to make fun of you, man." While Moms and Dad are in the back of the house after dinner, my brothers argue like they always seem to do when we're all in the same room. This time it's about sneakers. Ever since Aaron got his first real job cleaning the floors at Mr. Ray's, he acts like he's better than everybody. And his first pair of Jordan 11s went straight to his head.

"Bruh, you was just wearing the fakes last year," Markus points out with a sneaky smirk. "Why you actin' like them Air BALLS wasn't your favorite sneakers before you got *rich*?" DeShawn busts out laughing so hard apple juice sprays from his mouth water hose–style, soaking the front of Aaron's T-shirt.

"You lucky I don't like this shirt and Mama's close enough to hear you scream, Shawn." I watch all three of them laugh at Aaron's words, knowing he would never actually beat any of us up. Even if he wasn't in his new school clothes and new sneakers. Even if our parents weren't home. A question pops into my mind that flies out of my mouth before I can stop it.

"What about the people who don't have any jobs and no house and not many clothes but they wanna look nice like everybody else?" Everybody gets quiet. Aaron starts to answer right when Moms walks in with a look we're all scared of. We turned on the TV when she went back to her and Dad's room and forgot to turn it off before she came back out. We didn't hear her coming up the hall like we usually can always hear. None of us knows why we have an extra TV in the kitchen if she almost never lets us watch it.

"All of y'all are some fools if you think you gon' have this TV on right now," she says in the calm, scary way she says things when she wants us to know she's serious. Grabbing the remote, without even really looking down, she turns it off. Mom sorcery. "Rooms, homework, now." On his way out, Aaron tosses Moms an annoyed look that he knows she won't see. Markus poses behind her with his hand on his hip, trying to look just like she did when she walked into the kitchen. He stops and runs down the hall in just enough time for her to not catch him. DeShawn don't want no problems, so he's back in our room before both of them. Being the youngest means I can't get away that easy, and before I can get back there, too, I have to stick around to tell Moms about my first day. "And Aaron!"

"Yes, Ma?"

"My sweet, growing boy...please make sure you get in the tub. You smell like rotten apples, son. And you look like you been sweating for hours. Take care of that." Markus snickers from down the hall just before closing our bedroom door. "You too, Markus! You don't smell so clean, neither! That deodorant I bought y'all ain't for decoration. You supposed to *use* it. Y'all act like you can learn everything from YouTube but ain't tryna learn *that*," she screams behind them, knowing Markus can still hear her through the door. We can always hear Moms no matter where she is in our apartment.

I'm afraid she's going to ask me too much about my teachers and my classes and then—*gag*—about homework. And I can't just lie and pretend that my teacher didn't hop on his desk, rap about Chicago, and then give us an assignment that's gonna have the whole school making fun of me next week. Moms knows my nostrils get all big when I'm telling a lie. So I decide to be helpful and take the garbage out to the big dumpster near the back alley before she can even try to get me to spill.

DON'T GET ME WRONG...I LOVE MY MOMS, BUT I'M REALLY TIGHT WITH AARON, MARK, AND SHAWN.

 WE ALWAYS BE ARGUING AND JOKING, TOO, TALKING ABOUT SPORTS, AND EVEN FAKE SHOES.

BEING THE YOUNGEST CAN BE HARD SOMETIMES, BUT THEY ALL LOOK AFTER ME TO SEE IF I'M FINE.

BETWEEN THE JOKES WE BE CRACKIN', THE LAUGHS WE BE LAUGHIN',

THE LOVE WE ALL HAVE, YO, THAT'S NEVER LACKIN', THEM THE BROS!

I plop the heavy bag into the almost-full metal dumpster and stand on my tiptoes while I cram the top down onto it. Sometimes being size extra small really stinks.

Ha ha, stinks…garbage. You get it?

Our apartment doesn't really have much of a backyard, but there's this little wooden deck thing that's got a big pile of bikes and old sports equipment left behind by my brothers. I halfheartedly kick a deflated football that has MARKUS BARNES written in faded Sharpie on its side. Markus, DeShawn, and Aaron have no problem getting out in front of crowds of people to play sports, and Aaron is on his high school's debate team, meaning he gets extra credit basically for fighting with people on a stage. So why can't I get up and *talk* in front of anybody?

"My maaaaan," Dad says, walking around from the side door. "Are you really out here taking out the trash in this creepy ol' alley?" Dad gives me a look like somebody switched his son out for somebody else. "You *also* didn't have your usual second helping of your mama's lasagna. What's goin' on, son? Wanna talk about it?"

Most of the time Dad is pretty busy with work, keeping things together around the house, and volunteering around Creighton Park, but he always seems to know when something's up with me. Back when I was in the third grade, he once knew I was nervous about a test that was coming up because he saw me wiping off the kitchen table. None of us *ever* clean up stuff in the kitchen unless it's our turn. And wiping down the table after my brothers made a mess of it is the worst.

"Something happen at school today?"

"Something like that."

"Got a mean teacher? I need to roll up to the school and check somebody?"

"Nothing like that, Dad," I say, laughing a little at the thought of Dad coming up to my school to yell at my new teacher. For one, my dad's the nicest dude in the whole neighborhood. He's even super serious about how we catch mice and bugs around us and won't let any of us kill them if we can help it. Secondly, imagining Dad rolling up on the rapping teacher makes me think about when rappers battle each other. He'd definitely lose to Mr. James.

WELCOME TO THE BATTLE CALLED PARENTS VS.
    TEACHERS,
KIDS IN THE CROWD, SHOUTIN' LOUD FROM THE
    BLEACHERS.
THERE'S MR. JAMES, WITH HIS TIE AND HIS
    SNEAKERS,
WHILE DAD WORE HIS WORK BOOTS, THAT
    COULDN'T BE WEAKER!

JAMES STRIKES FIRST WITH A JOKE IN HIS
    VERSE.
HE CALLS DAD OLD, AND OHHHH, THAT ONE
    HURTS!
BUT DAD COMES BACK WITH A PUNCH JUST THE
    SAME
WHEN HE CALLS MR. JAMES REAL CORNY AND
    LAME.

THE CROWD GOES WILD--SO DAD'S FEELIN'
   PROUD,
BUT JAMES HAS A LINE THAT'LL TAKE HIM OFF
   HIS CLOUD.

THE SCORE'S TIED NOW, BUT IT'S COMIN' TO AN
   END,
SO WHOEVER MAKES THE FANS GO CRAZY NEXT,
   WINS.

LET'S JUST SAY, MR. JAMES DOESN'T PLAY
WHEN HE DROPS THE NEXT BOMB ON MY DAD
   THAT DAY!
THE CROWD GOES CRAY! AND MY DAD SAYS,

   "HEY,
THIS WAS A GREAT BATTLE THAT WE HAD, MR. J!"

"I—I got all these raps and rhymes and things to say in my head, Dad. But when it comes time to talk out loud, like at school and stuff, I get too nervous. Like, I-might-throw-up-on-somebody-type nervous. And my hands get gross and sweaty and I feel kind of dizzy and all the other kids start giving me the side-eye, and..." Dad raises his hands like he's trying to stop traffic in the middle of a

super-busy street. Maybe he really is. I feel like I'm
in a car speeding down a highway headed for a
crash next week.

"Whoa, Simon, whoa! Hold up and breathe,
son," Dad says, smiling and putting his arm around
my shoulder. It makes me feel the same way when
Moms squeezes my hand. *Not in public, obviously.*
And this time we aren't in the school parking lot.
We're alone in the alley by ourselves. So I guess
Notorious D.O.G. can let this slide.

"What's this all about? Y'all already got some kind of show comin' up at Booker T.? It's only y'all's first day!"

"No, Dad. But my new teacher, Mr. James, is making us do these oral presentation things. And I got picked to go first," I tell him, feeling like this is partially his fault. *It's because of you that my last name is Barnes.* Forever cursed to be called first. Ha! That rhymed.

"Aw, snap. And what's it got to be on?"

"He said something *timely*. Something important going on in Creighton Park." This is already getting old. I shrug and shake my head, looking away, half wishing how sad I look would make Dad feel sorry enough to do my assignment for me. I lay on the Simon Sad Face extra thick.

"And you get to pick your topic?"

"Uh, yeah."

"That's tight!" Sometimes Dad tries to be cool and uses slang when I just want him to save me from school.

"Dad!"

"Did I ever tell you about my eighth-grade talent show?"

"You were in a talent show?" My dad's great, but he's not exactly the talent show type. He's a mechanic who repairs air-conditioning and heating systems around the city. If anybody asked any of us, we'd all say his greatest talent is fixing anything broken around the house. But getting up onstage to sing or dance? Nah. Not Dad.

"Yup. Me and your uncle Richie decided we'd sing the song from this popular TV show *The Fresh Prince of Bel-Air*—you ever seen it?"

"Yeah, Mom makes me watch it with her sometimes. He's the one with all the funny hats who went to live with his rich uncle, right? He had to wear one of those nerdy uniforms to school and he turned the jacket inside out, right?" The more I think about it, the more I remember how cool I thought the theme song was, wishing I could rhyme like that.

"That's right, that's the one! Your uncle Richie was supposed to handle the singing, and I was going to do some kind of crazy basketball tricks, Harlem

Globetrotter–style, you know?" Dad laughs. I knew he didn't get up there to sing. That would have been tragic. Still, imagining Dad onstage spinning multiple basketballs at the same time the way he once told me that group did still seems like a bad joke.

"Are you serious right now, Dad?"

"Oh yeah. We had these matching tracksuits and everything. Thought we were fly and were gon' impress *all* the ladies." The thought of Dad trying to impress all the ladies is the weirdest thing. *Gag.*

"Move along, Dad."

"Hey, hey, I got your mom, didn't I?"

"Come on!"

"All right, all right. Anyway, long story short, the talent show was a mess. Richie forgot the words to the song, even though he had sung it a million times. I dropped two basketballs off the stage, one of which hit our principal in the face and broke her glasses." Hilarious. Ms. Berry would throw a whole fit if somebody hit her in the face with a basketball. Dad puts his hand over his forehead, like he can still feel the embarrassment.

"For real? So what happened then?"

"Nothing. And that's my point, Simon. Richie and I got up there and embarrassed ourselves, but nobody cared. By a few days later, everybody at school was already talking about something else. So you see, there's nothing to be scared of, son. You'll get up in front of the class and you'll do your thing. You'll be okay." Dad puts his hand out to shake my hand.

"Yeah, maybe you're right, I guess." I'm not sure if I really mean it or not, but Dad has a way of, at least, making me feel like I won't be the first person in history to embarrass myself. I still can't believe he and Uncle Richie actually tried something like that in front of the *whole* school—never mind their class. *Maybe I have some of that in me.*

"So, what's your topic gon' be? Your mom told me to ask you about all this, but don't tell her I told you," he says, as he eyeballs me so I don't rat him out. He's always on a mission for my mom, and a lot of times it kinda works.

"Well, you know Sunny, the guy who's always sweeping our street? I don't think he has any real place to live. He got me thinking about all the homeless people in Creighton Park," I say. But that's as far as I've gotten. All the people without homes in Creighton Park.

"You might be onto something, son," Dad says, patting my back and looking up into the sky. "You might be onto something *big.*"

TUESDAY

CHAPTER 7

THE NEXT DAY, MR. JAMES COLLECTS THE
work sheets he gave us at the end of class yesterday,
describing the topics we've each picked for our presentations. I scribbled down the thought I shared
with Dad, still not feeling like I know enough to
talk about it in front of my class. But I can't start
off on the wrong foot by not doing this first assignment, so I did what Moms always says when she
tells me *Go with your gut, baby.* Minus the baby
part.

"Homelessness. Wow, Simon. That's major."
I secretly wish people would stop saying that. It

doesn't feel good, and the thought of how major it is gives me the bubble guts. "Looking forward to Monday." *Gurgle.* Mr. James smiles as he runs his eyes up and down my work sheet before moving on to the next kid. He seems excited and looks like he really believes I could do a good job, but all I hear is the word *Monday. Monday!* As in six days away Monday. There's only been one Monday so far, and that was just yesterday. I still don't see why any kid has to present the second week of school. Aren't we supposed to be doing fun stuff like playing games to get to know each other and talking about what we did all summer? But I have to be ready. What would Notorious D.O.G. do?

I NEED TO BE CONFIDENT, I NEED TO BE BOLD,
I NEED TO SHOW THE WORLD THAT MY STYLE IS
   COLD.
IT'S THE D.O.G., THEY GON' HEAR ME BARK.
NOT THE SIZE OF THE DOG, IT'S ABOUT THE
   HEART.
SEE, I KNOW I'M SMART, AND MY RHYMES ARE
   SICK,

AND I KNOW PEOPLE GON' LISTEN WHEN I SPIT.
SO I NEED TO BE CONFIDENT, NEED TO BE BOLD,
NEED TO SHOW THE WHOLE WORLD THAT MY
    STYLE IS COLD.
WOOF WOOF!

At lunch, Maria is telling me and C.J. about her hundred-year-old cat, Diego Rivera. He seems like a regular old cat to me, but Maria thinks he has some kind of special powers or something. Her eyes get all big, poking like they're gonna pop right out of her head as she explains his "powers" and tries to convince me and C.J. that he worked magic right in front of her one day before church.

"Anyway, right when it was time for us to go, I couldn't find the shiny black shoes Tía Laura bought for me anywhere. I looked under my bed, in the closet, and even in the trash can just in case somebody was playing games with me." Maria always thinks this. "Then I hear a *meow-meow-meow* coming from the couch. I got down on my hands and knees and he was sitting there licking my shoes! Isn't that craaazy?" Ri-Ri smiles and bites into a carrot stick, waiting for us to react. I'm waiting for the rest of the story, but it never comes.

"Mmm, yeah, craaazy," C.J. says back right before he lets out a classic C.J. yawn that sounds like a bear who's just waking up from hibernation. "I wonder what else he can do. Maybe ol' Diego can make my homework magically disappear? Everybody says their dog ate their homework, but what if your cat's breath could turn mine into dust?"

"You think you're so funny, C.J. But Diego doesn't help lazy kids," Maria says, rolling her eyes. We both pass our milks over to C.J. even though me and him don't have fruit to exchange with Maria. Today's menu is hard slices of sausage pizza, a chocolate milk, and a crusty oatmeal raisin cookie. Of course the food makes Maria go off about how that *has* to be what she talks about for her oral presentation. She starts telling us her idea, and C.J.'s eyes get big for real this time, looking behind me. I turn to see what he's looking at and see Bobby Sanchez flop around into the backs of a few kids just before landing on me, spilling his carton of chocolate milk onto my tray. Instead of him trying to stop it, he turns to look at me while he holds the carton upside down over my food until nothing but drops comes out.

"Oops, sorry, Barnes," Bobby says, in a way that means he isn't even a little bit sorry. "Saw you handing your milk over to CiCi over here so I thought you might need some more."

"It's C.J., bruh," C.J. jabs back, looking at Bobby as if he smells funny.

"Whatever." He kind of does.

"Got enough milk now, baby Simon?" Bobby laughs and high-fives Victor, his forever sidekick, who always laughs at Bobby's jokes even when they aren't that funny. Even though the joke was majorly corny, my face feels hot and I get so mad I can't even move. Bobby stands there for a minute waiting for me to maybe scream or cry in front of everybody, but

I just sit there feeling my cold, stained T-shirt stick to my chest and goose bumps rising all over me. I stare at my tray and the slice of pizza I was gonna eat just before Bobby turned it into a muddy flood in a mushy pizza yard. Under the table, Maria kicks my shoe and waits for me to say something back. I open my mouth, ready to ask Bobby if that was the same shirt he had on last year. Then I open it again, ready to tell him he shouldn't have skipped his shower this morning. All the perfect comebacks are in my head. I just have to…I just have to…

BOBBY SANCHEZ, YOU'RE THE MEANEST—I MEAN
   IT!
YOUR BREATH'S KINDA FUNKY, AND YOUR SHIRT'S
   NOT THE CLEANEST.
YOU ALWAYS PICKIN' ON ME CUZ I'M SMALL…
   BUT YOU SMELL.
WE DON'T SAY NOTHING 'BOUT IT, WE JUST KEEP
   IT TO OURSELVES.
 YOU'RE THE TYPE OF KID WHO DOESN'T KNOW
   WHEN TO QUIT…
DOESN'T KNOW WHEN TO STOP, DOESN'T KNOW
   WHEN TO SIT.

SO IF YOU GET BULLIED, IT'LL ALL MAKE SENSE
AND WE'LL ALL BE HAPPY CUZ...THAT'S WHAT
YOU GET!

"You...uhh...you so..."

"*Uhhh, uuuuh,* what, shorty? Oh man, definitely time for you to go back to kindergarten with all the other little babies!" Bobby says as he walks away from our table just before any teachers can see what he's done.

"Here's some napkins, Simon." Maria pushes a pile over to me, trying to help me dry up. "You want some of my plátanos? I'm not that hungry and that pizza looked like plastic anyway." I'm not even hungry anymore, but I take a plátano and hold it in my hand while C.J. goes to dump my milky tray.

"Sorry, Simon. Those guys are the worst," C.J. grumbles as he sits back down. He breaks off a piece of what's left of his pizza and slides it over to me on a napkin. I still can't open my mouth. How am I going to eat anything?

"Yeah, don't worry about them, Simon." Maria pats my back the way Ms. Estelle does sometimes when she wants us to feel better but doesn't know what to say. "Bobby's just mad because you always look cooler than him. Can't let him mess with you like that. Remember: *Think positive. Be positive.*"

"You got that off a poster in your uncle's office?"

"Hey, how'd you know that?" Maria says as we pack up for recess. I just shiver, hoping by the end of recess my new T-shirt will be dry.

After school Markus is laid out on the couch again with his feet dangling off the edge when the lock turns on the front door. Neither of us is expecting anybody for a few more hours, so we know whoever is on the other side is about to catch us red-handed—Markus scrolling the internet on his new phone that Dad got him for emergencies and me with my arm elbow-deep in the box of Fruity-O's. Dad smiles and shakes his head at us as he walks in. I can't lie with rainbow crumbs all over my face, and Markus's backpack is too far away to pretend he was working on his math.

"Party time's over, y'all." Markus swings his feet

off the couch edge and grumbles under his breath, walking over to the kitchen, where I'm already washing my hands and putting the box back on top of the refrigerator. "I'm not gon' take your little phone away from you, but I'ma be calling in an hour and you better pick up. I'll expect an update on today's assignment over the phone, too. I got the email from your math teacher so I know what you supposed to be doin'," Dad warns Markus as he pulls his hundred-pound textbooks out onto the counter. *Sheesh!* These teachers are doing *way* too much!

"Simon, let's go." Dad says this like I know what he's talking about. Up until a few minutes ago, I didn't even know he'd be home this early.

"Y-y-you don't want me to do my homework like Markus?"

"This *is* your homework."

What?

"I was thinking about your project and I got a little surprise for you. A special place for us to visit—just you and me." Now I'm *really* nervous. I hear Markus laugh in his seat. I know math couldn't be that funny, so he's definitely laughing at the Notorious D.O.G. "I think your idea is great." Oh boy. "Figured you should talk to some of the people you want to do your project on. People like Sunny."

"We're going to the park?"

"Even better. To the shelter. We're going to serve food." I thought knowing about Sunny would be enough. Suddenly I feel extra nervous. All this time all I was thinking about was having to talk in front of my class. But I never thought about who I'd have to talk *to* before I got to that part. "But first, put on a clean shirt, my boy. Looks like you missed your whole mouth at lunch."

"This kind of sounds like work, Dad," I say, walking beside him toward the corner. But I feel bad about my words as soon as they come out of my mouth. Because Dad is right. I have to meet more people who don't have homes if I'm going to learn what their life is like. He laughs and slows down a little. For every step Dad takes, I have to take like five.

"I mean, that sounds cool," I say, touching Dad's hand for a second before letting it go. We are out in public and all. The Notorious D.O.G. doesn't hold hands with his dad!

When me and Dad get to the corner of Loving Street and Linden Boulevard, I notice we're still on the side of Creighton where the park is. On the other side of Booker T. Except we're across the street. We make a left on Linden and stand in front of a building that looks just like all the other buildings on the block, dark brown and made of brick with bars on the windows. Water drips from an air conditioner above the front door, and for a minute I think we're going to somebody's house.

"All right, we're here," Dad announces.

The only thing that makes me believe we're actually at a homeless shelter is the sign right outside the door that says CREIGHTON PARK COMMUNITY OUTREACH: OPEN HEARTS, OPEN DOORS. Dad and I walk in, stopping at the front desk, where an older lady with a funny wig on says "Welcome back" to my dad and "Hello" to me. This is one of the places that keeps Dad busy and I never knew it was right down the street, right behind my school. The lady comes around the desk to shake my hand.

"This must be Simon. My name is Wanda. I'm glad you're here." It feels strange that she already knows my name, but Dad smiles at her and gives me *the look*. The *don't you embarrass me in here* look.

"Hi, Miss Wanda," I say back, shaking her hand. Miss Wanda smells like fancy oils and peppermints just like Grandma Lucille so I guess she's all right. She grabs a visitor pass sticker off the counter, writes my name on it, and sticks it to my chest.

"Everybody is gon' be so excited to meet you, Simon. And y'all are just in time for dinner service. You can go on and head to the kitchen and wash up. There's somebody there who will give you your apron and get you all set up. Your dad knows most of how things go around here," she tells me, giving me a wink. Aprons. Rules. *Dinner*. My mouth gets all watery until I remember the dinner isn't for me.

In the kitchen upstairs, I learn that volunteers are in charge of handing out food to the people who come to the shelter for a free meal and that we need to wear plastic gloves for germs. Dad's going to stand behind a big bowl of mashed potatoes and serve spoonfuls out to people in the cafeteria line. I'm in charge of bringing rolls and little foil-wrapped packs of butter to everyone at their tables.

When I think about people being homeless, I think of Sunny. And since Sunny's old, I'm surprised to see so many differ-ent kinds of people who show up needing food. There are old people like Grandma Lucille, moms who look sorta like my mom, and a lot of them have kids with them who don't look much older or younger than me. I even see teenagers

who look like they could have been my big brother Aaron's friends. It makes me feel sad that all these people don't have money to buy their own food or a kitchen to cook at home in.

I'm so busy on bread roll patrol that I almost don't see Sunny sitting at a table near the back of the dining hall. I walk up to him and he smiles at me, hard, through all his missing teeth.

"Rhymin' Simon, I thought that might be you!" Sunny says, still cheesin' hard. "Are you and your dad helping with all the dinner stuff they got goin' on in here? That's mighty kind of you." I wonder how Sunny could bite down into the stale roll so hard when it looks like he only has five good teeth. I watch him roll the wet piece of bread around in his mouth with his tongue a few seconds before remembering to say something back. Why didn't Sunny get dentures like Grandma Lucille? It looks like he's needed them for a *long* time now.

"Wassup, Sunny," I say, suddenly feeling awkward to be standing there talking to him by myself. "Yeah, Dad brought me here to volunteer. And I'm actually doing an assignment for school." I want to tell him it's about him being homeless, but I suddenly feel strange about telling him that to his face. I don't know if he'd still want to talk to me. Sunny's basically been watching me grow up since I was like seven years old, but I've barely ever talked to him before this. It feels rude to tell him that, all of a sudden, I want to know why he doesn't really live anywhere the way I do.

"And you want to ask us some questions?" Sunny's smile gets bigger. Like he's been waiting for this and is proud of himself for being able to read my mind.

"Well, just you...if it's okay. I don't want to bother you while you eat your dinner, though," I say, not feeling ready. I don't even really know the first thing to say.

"Oh yeah! Probably got too many meetings tonight, but I think my schedule will free up a little bit later this week," he jokes. "For real, though, kiddo, it's not a bother at all. Come back tomorrow after school and I'll holla at ya."

WEDNESDAY

CHAPTER 8

"COME ON, C.J.! I DON'T WANNA MISS
Sunny!" Sometimes C.J. can be the slowest kid in
the world. It's already Wednesday afternoon, so
my report is due in just five days. I practically drag
C.J. down to the sidewalk, where Aaron is already
sucked into his phone, waiting for us.

"Yeah, come on, both of y'all," Aaron says, pulling his backpack higher up on his shoulder. He jets
down the sidewalk, barely checking to see if we're
with him or not. He agreed to take me and C.J.
to the shelter, mostly because he can shoot hoops
with his friends at Locust Court afterward. "Gotta

practice as much as possible," he said last night when Dad and I asked if he could take me.

As we get closer to the corner of Locust and Loving Streets, I smile, thinking about last night. Handing out rolls and then helping out with dessert was actually kinda fun. Sunny had a lot of friends in there who I kept overhearing talk about *the good old days*. I wondered, since they're all homeless, if it was okay to be joking around with them. They were joking with each other and Sunny always has something goofy to say, but I still felt like maybe I should be more serious around him. Maybe joking with him would make it feel like I was making fun of him. I don't know. Maybe I'll ask him about that today.

I'M NOT REALLY SURE HOW TO ACT AROUND
   SUNNY,
DON'T WANT TO BE RUDE, THINKIN' I'M BEING
   FUNNY.
   I'D HATE TO EMBARRASS HIM IN FRONT OF HIS
   FRIENDS
OR BY ACCIDENT, THEN HE WON'T SPEAK TO ME
   AGAIN!

SO I'LL PLAY IT COOL, TALK LESS, LISTEN MORE,

CUZ THAT'S THE WHOLE REASON THAT I'M GOIN'

HERE FOR,

TO LEARN WHAT THIS MAN'S GOT TO SAY ABOUT

HIS LIFE.

CHILL OUT, SIMON, EVERYTHING'S GONNA BE

AIGHT!

"Hey, Simon, think they'll have a vending machine with some good snacks in there? I'm starving!"

"You ain't starving, C.J." Aaron answers for me, overhearing C.J. from steps ahead of us. "It's a homeless shelter. You know, for people who actually *need* food. Don't think they gon' be too worried about showing you where a vending machine is at, bruh."

"Chill, we'll eat after we get out of here."

Miss Wanda walks me, Aaron, and C.J. over to a big room that's full of tables with chairs, some comfy old couches, and a Ping-Pong table in the corner.

A super-sad-looking rec room with not enough light. No one's playing Ping-Pong, but there's some kids working on a big puzzle at one table and some adults reading magazines on the couches.

"All right, boys, holler if you need anything," Miss Wanda says as she waves her hand toward the table where Sunny's waiting for us. We start walking over and Aaron finds a corner to sit in and forget about us while he texts on his phone. Even though it's only Sunny who I told I was coming back today, Miss Wanda has set things up real official for the Notorious D.O.G. For a second, it makes me feel like I might know what to say when I sit down with him. Maybe.

"Rhymin' Simon and your boy C.J.!" Sunny says, saying our names like it's part of a song. "Sit down, sit down."

At first, I feel funny asking Sunny questions. I look down at my notebook, where I wrote five questions because Mr. James told me I should be prepared. I feel nervous about talking like that to an old man I don't really know, besides the fact that he's always somewhere around my block, and

I don't want to make him feel funny by getting all up in his business. But before I even get to question one, C.J. and Sunny start talking about a blues band that C.J.'s uncle Lou played in sometimes.

"Oh boy, they can play, can't they? You know I used to sing with a band sometimes, back when I was a younger man," Sunny says, looking proud. "Used to run around here doin' all kinds of little jobs, too."

"Oh yeah?" I lean in. It's funny imagining Sunny as someone who used to look like me or my brothers a long time ago. Grandma Lucille looks like she's been a granny forever. Sunny telling me and C.J. he was a kid in Creighton Park, Chicago, feels like something that couldn't be real.

"When I was y'all's age, I used to make extra cash shoveling snow off sidewalks. Wasn't no allowance or funny stuff like that, so I had to make my *own* money," Sunny says, making me think about how my brothers do that sometimes in the winters, too. "I had to get out there, roll up my sleeves, and do real work! Didn't have no video games and internet this and that keeping me all up in the house staring at a screen. My mama barely let me get caught up listening to the radio too much." Sunny had a mama who wouldn't let him chill, either. I pause for a second imagining him in the kitchen and somebody older than him telling him *Rooms, homework, now.*

"Now the whole world got they faces glued to they little gadgets and machines and don't know what it's like to go out and earn your money for real. The internet's taking over everything, I tell you." C.J. and I just stare. Sunny sounds like Grandma Lucille with a deeper voice and long gray hairs that grow out of his nose like weeds. But his hands wave all over the place when he gets excited the exact same way hers do.

"Got my first real job at eighteen straight out of high school. Gave that place fifteen good years of my life till they dumped me, man," he says, his voice lowering and kind of slowing down. I want to ask him what the job was and what happened, but Sunny starts looking out at nothing after telling us he lost his job.

"Hey, Sunny," C.J. says, smiling. "Will you sing a song for us? Since you used to sing in a band

and all." C.J.'s timing is always kind of off. He's not the biggest on manners, but this time I think he's trying to make Sunny feel better. I'm glad because the look on Sunny's face makes me feel like I don't know what to do.

"You don't have to ask me twice." Sunny stands up, clears his throat, and starts to sing the same song I heard him singing the other day in front of our apartment building. The one about the sunny side of the street.

When Sunny sings, it feels like his voice takes over the whole room. And I see a whole bunch of people turn around and stare at him from their seats. He sounds like something off the radio. But from like fifty years ago, of course. I've never heard anything like that in real life. For a minute I forget where we are. That this guy is going off like this in a homeless shelter rec room. I snap out of it and look around when the whole room starts clapping at the end of Sunny's song.

I look up at the clock on the wall and realize it's almost time for Aaron to walk us home. I haven't asked Sunny all of my questions for my project, but

I hope I have enough to not sound completely lost on Monday when I have to present. I decide to ask question number five from my list.

"Sunny, can I ask you one more thing before we have to leave?" I say, holding my pencil in my hand, ready to write down as much as I can.

"Shoot, Rhymin' Simon."

"Okay, what's one thing you want people to know about being homeless? Or, you know, something people might not know." I stumble over my words a little, feeling embarrassed to use that word and for the fact that I've only ever come here for a project. Sunny just smiles and looks down at his hands.

"That's easy, young man. I wish people knew we're not invisible. People walk by and pretend I don't exist. And I know they have their reasons, but it hurts. Let me ask you something, Simon. Have you ever felt like people don't see or hear you?"

I nod, not knowing what to say. I thought I would be the only one asking the questions. That how Sunny feels has nothing to do with me.

"Thanks, Sunny." Something inside me feels

happy for coming but kind of low at the same time. What Sunny said sounded a lot like how I feel sometimes, but it seemed kinda wrong to compare myself to him. I don't have to live the way he does. I don't have it as bad. I say thank you again while C.J. teaches Sunny how to dap him up. We walk over to Aaron to snap him back into reality, and as he walks us out of the rec room, Sunny calls my name.

"Hey, Simon! Now that I sang for you, you owe us a little something. I've heard all about you, son. Time to let the rest of the hood hear your talents."

"Yeah, Notorious D.O.G.," C.J. agrees, cracking himself up. "Time to let out that big ol' bark!" He even barks, like I'm some kind of joke.

"Yeah...aight...next time. I gotchu."

THURSDAY

CHAPTER 9

"YOU KNOW HOW SUNNY BE SINGING IN the street all the time?" Five minutes after the recess bell rings, the three of us are at our spot. The swing set farthest from the building with the wood chips. It's the most boring part of the school yard, but it's just right for us since nobody else hangs out here.

"Yeah! He be like *shoooo-DOOP!*" Maria yells from up above us just before flying backward on the middle swing. C.J. and I crack up at Maria's attempt at old-folks singing. C.J. leans against the swing post and uses his elbow to shove Maria forward again while I chill back on the swing next to hers.

"Happiest homeless dude I ever seen," C.J. adds, Cheeto crumbs flying through his teeth. "I thought having no real house to live in was sad. But Sunny seems like he's happy all the time."

"Yeah, he stood up in front of everybody and sang that song he always be singing when he sweeps leaves around my house. And then he said he wanted to hear ME."

"Whaaat?" Maria flies off the rubber seat in midair with open arms and walks back in between me and C.J., reaching out to slow the swing so she can sit. "He did all that? My tío Phillip does that sometimes when we go over to his and Tía Laura's house for dinner. It's kinda corny but him and Tía look so mushy dancing around the kitchen holding each other all close and stuff," Maria explains with a big smile on her face. "With the salsa playing and the pernil in the oven, everybody is so happy. That's how it was in the shelter? Did you rap? They had pernil in there?" Maria always asks one million questions at the same time when she gets excited

and always wants to know if people eat the same food she eats at her house.

"I don't know about no *pair-knee*, but they had chicken. He sang a whole song and then everybody clapped for him. For a minute I forgot he was homeless." I feel bad for thinking this. But I don't ever hear people saying good things about the people I see living on the streets. Adults always act like we gotta walk faster when they see them and make sure, no matter what, we don't touch them or else we might catch some type of cooties. I mean, they do be stinkin', but after talking to Sunny at the shelter more than I usually do, something feels wrong about looking at him like that.

I GET IT...SOMETIMES HOMELESS PEOPLE
    SMELL
BUT THAT DOESN'T MEAN WE SHOULDN'T TREAT
    THEM WELL.
THEY GOT FEELINGS, TOO, AND THEY WANT TO BE
    SEEN
SO IT REALLY DOESN'T MATTER IF THEIR
    CLOTHES AIN'T CLEAN.

TAKE SUNNY—I LIKE HIM, CUZ HE'S SO NICE
AND I'VE LEARNED A LOT ABOUT HIM, SINCE I'VE
  SEEN HIM TWICE.
AT THE SHELTER, HE WAS TELLIN' ME 'BOUT HIS
  LIFE.
I JUST WISH ALL ADULTS WOULD TAKE MOMS'
  ADVICE:

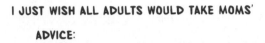

"TREAT OTHERS LIKE YOU WANT TO BE TREATED."

C.J. shoots his empty Cheeto bag into a trash can next to the swings, wiping the front and back of his fingers on his jeans. Red dust everywhere. His mama is gon' be mad but she's probably used to it by now.

"My pops says we shouldn't talk to bums on the street."

"Homeless people," Maria and I say at the same time.

For a minute C.J. looks embarrassed. "You know what I mean. Bu—homeless people always be askin' for money. Pops says they don't never use that money for anything but they always asking. He says kids shouldn't be talkin' to grown folks on the street, anyway." We all get quiet for a second. Sunny never asked me for any money. And he looked so happy sitting at his table when everybody was eating their food. When people give Sunny money for food, I think he uses it for food.

"Sunny told me that hurts his—"

"Wow! I can't believe it. Big Head Barnes actually talks!" Bobby and his sidekicks crash into me like they didn't see me standing here, almost appearing out of thin air. But I'm the first one Bobby calls out. They look back and forth between each other and laugh. "Continue your little story, shorty. No need to get quiet. We want to hear it, too. Pretend we're not even here." Bobby stands to my right only a few inches away, towering over me. Pretending

he's not here ain't even possible. I wish he wasn't, though. "Hellooo, anybody in there? Or are you too stupid to understand what I'm saying?" I keep my eyes low. The bad part about having our own spot on the playground is that we're just far enough for the teachers to miss things. Like how Bobby's arm suddenly around my shoulders don't mean he's suddenly my friend.

"Oh, shut up, Bobby! Don't you have anything better to do?" Maria stands just as close as Bobby now but on the left side of me.

ALL THIS ACTION? THINGS GON' HAPPEN!
VICTOR, JUSTIN, RIGHT THERE LAUGHIN',
BOBBY'S MOCKIN', C.J.'S WATCHIN',
RI--RI'S MAD, SO SHE STARTS TALKIN'.

 I WISH I COULD GET TO WALKIN'
OR SPEAK UP, BUT THAT'S NO OPTION
SO I'M PLOTTIN', THINKIN', PLANNIN',
FEEL LIKE SCREAMIN', BUT I'M STANDIN'...STILL.

THINGS JUST FEEL TOO REAL.
I WANNA DIP, I WANNA PEEL,

I REALLY WANNA LEAVE THIS SCENE.
THEN BOBBY WOULDN'T BE SO MEAN!

I KNOW MY HEAD'S THE BIGGEST SHAPE
BUT ALL OF US HAVE THINGS WE HATE
ABOUT OURSELVES, THAT WE WOULD FIX
IF WE KNEW MAGIC, OR SOME TRICKS.

AND I WOULD STAND ON FIFTY STICKS
IF IT WOULD MAKE ME SIX FOOT SIX.
I'M HAPPY FOR MY FRIENDS WHO HELP
BUT I WISH I COULD DEFEND MYSELF!
WOOF!

I wish I could say something. Anything. But it's like my voice climbed back down into my throat and is splashing its legs around in my stomach. Plus, I don't want no drama. It's only the first week of school!

"What's better than hanging out with Stuck on Stupid over here? The little guy makes me laugh." Bobby squeezes tighter and takes a look over his right shoulder toward the school building, flashing a smile at Mrs. Leary. Mrs. Leary smiles back, adding a clueless wave.

"Look who's talking," Maria says. "The main one calling names should probably be in recess study hall asking for extra credit right *now*. I don't even know how you made it to the fifth grade, Bobby." Bobby's smirk drops along with his arm. "Don't think I forgot about how you had to repeat kindergarten at Bell." Bobby's sidekicks start to giggle until he elbows one of them in the stomach and snaps his fingers at them. They turn and follow behind him like puppies as he starts to walk away.

"You better watch yourself. Might get hurt talking to me like that."

"Yo! I ain't never seen Bobby Sanchez lookin' like that! That was CRAZY, Maria!" C.J. says. Maria dusts fake dirt off her shoulders, looking proud, and we all bust out laughing. "He didn't know what to say after that stuff about kindergarten!"

"Yeah, how'd you know all that?" I knew Bobby looked too big to be in the same grade as us. But I always brushed it off, thinking it was just me that was too small. Just like how I feel right now. I can't believe somebody had to say something for me again. I know Maria and C.J. are my squad and all, but I wish I knew what to say when Bobby comes around. Or when everybody's staring at me waiting for me to speak. I just don't want to say anything stupid. I don't want everybody to see when I say the wrong thing. I feel like I know all the right words when I'm rhymin', but that's different...right?

"You know my mama used to work in the school office. I hear stuff," Maria says, staring at me for too long. "But Simon. Why didn't you say anything? It was like you weren't even here. You gotta say something back to that fool or he's gonna keep tryna play you." The bell rings and we all head back into the building.

It was like I wasn't even here. Like I was invisible. Like Sunny. But Sunny's not really invisible. People just treat him like he is. But when he sings... everybody knows he's there. Everybody. Maybe the same can happen for me.

CHAPTER 10

IT DOESN'T MATTER THAT MR. JAMES IS
talking about the scariest thing ever. No matter
what, he makes it seem like doing an oral presentation is the coolest, walking around the room asking
us all kinds of serious questions that sound way
too deep so early in the school year. *Who IS this
guy and WHERE did he come from?* It's only been
three days, but I've already learned that he does
this thing where he asks a question, stops in front
of somebody's desk, and smiles at them until they
say something. Today it's me.

"Think about it, scholars," he says, touching his

bright red bow tie. "What is something you see all the time—and you think you know about it, but not really? Like, if someone asked you how it all got started, would you be able to tell them?" He pauses in front of my desk, smiling all corny at me while he kneels down to look me in the eye. "What don't you know about the man you wrote about on your topic sheet? How did he get there?" I bust out laughing. Being put on the spot makes me feel awkward and I start cracking up. I don't know if Mr. James wants me to say something back or if this is still a part of his speech. I laugh some more, looking around, waiting for him to walk over to somebody else. He knocks on my desk with his fist two times before he keeps walking. "Think about it."

Maria turns and shoots me a look, then crosses her eyes while sticking her tongue out at me. It looks even

funnier when she does it because of her pink glasses and the fact that Mr. James can't see his best student scrunching up her face behind his back, looking like a cross-eyed fool and a smiley Mr. James twin. I cover my mouth before I lose control. Mr. James weaves in between a few more desks, finishing his speech, and the thoughts in my brain get too loud for me to hear anything else. *What don't I know about Sunny?* I start to write some stuff on a sheet Mr. James gives us for notes. *Maybe I should write some stuff I already know. Yeah, I'll do that.*

SUNNY IS A COOL DUDE WHO GREW UP IN THIS
HOOD.

HE WAS IN A BAND, CUZ HE SANG REALLY GOOD.

HE SHOVELED SIDEWALKS AS A KID TO MAKE
MONEY.

NOW HE SWEEPS SIDEWALKS, AIN'T LIFE KINDA
FUNNY?

HAD HIS FIRST REAL JOB WHEN HE WAS
EIGHTEEN,

DOESN'T LIKE THE INTERNET (HE KINDA HATES
SCREENS),
WEARS BAGGY JEANS, HIS CLOTHES AIN'T TOO
CLEAN,

BUT HE'S JUST LIKE US, CUZ HE WANTS TO BE
SEEN!

SUNNY'S REAL FUNNY, HE JOKES WITH HIS
FRIENDS.
HE MAKES PEOPLE LAUGH, AND EVERYBODY
GRINS.

HE'S BROWN LIKE A PENNY, TALL, AND HE'S
SKINNY
AND HE'S USUALLY UPBEAT WHEN I SEE HIM ON
THE STREET!

That's a lot! I think. I mean, I don't want to be
all up in Sunny's business anyway. Moms and Dad
always tell me I need to stay out of *grown folks'
business*, and Sunny is *the* grownest. He's like one
million years old. Besides, wouldn't getting in his
business even more make him feel bad? Last time
I saw him, he started to look a little sad before he

started to sing. Just after he told me he lost his old job. Mr. James starts to blur out even more as I remember the look on Sunny's face, until I realize I've been holding my pee for *way* too long, having staredowns with Mr. James about *timely* things. It's about *time* I go handle that before the Notorious D.O.G. soaks his seat.

One of the first things Mr. James told us on Monday—besides the fact that we're gonna do the scariest thing ever—is that being in fifth grade means we don't have to raise our hands to go to the bathroom anymore. As long as there's a pass, we can go handle our business, because he trusts us, he says. I spot the bright red hall pass dangling from the hook that matches Mr. James's favorite bow tie, nailed into the wall next to the door, and hop out of my seat as fast as I can just in case somebody else is close to peeing on themselves, too. Luckily Bobby isn't around to try funny stuff, and Maria's face is almost glued into her work sheet with her pencil flying down the page. I slip out of the door before Mr. James has a chance to smile at me again.

I don't know how he knows we're going to have such a great year when he just met us.

The fifth-grade hallway of Booker T. feels so big when nobody's in it and it takes forever to get to the bathroom at the other end. The walls are made of an ugly green shiny tile with pictures of kids in classrooms learning stuck all over them. I ain't never seen kids look that happy to be here. And I didn't know any of those kids. Teachers' voices boom all loud through the walls about homework and assignments and rules. What's weird is that nobody else is out here with me, but I guess it's because, besides this being the fifth-grade hall, it's where the main office is. Too easy to get caught and too easy to get sent there if you get in trouble. A good chance somebody could see me on the way to the bathroom.

"What do you *mean* you don't have another number we can use? There's got to be another one, Robert. It's too early in the school year for these kinds of games, young man." I hear this loud voice boom before I see it, and I know it's coming from the principal's office because it's the only door that's always wide open when we're supposed to be in class. "Now I'm going to ask you one more time. Is there another number we can use to contact your father? We need to speak to him immediately." Then nothing. Just before I reach the door that says BOYS on it, I see Bobby sitting in a chair across from Principal Berry's desk with his head down, staring at his fingers even though he doesn't have anything on them. "Go on about your business, Simon." Principal Berry's voice cuts at me before I even notice I'm walking too slow in front of the door. Bobby's neck pops up and he gives me a look just before I remember the Notorious D.O.G. can't pee on himself.

In the empty bathroom surrounded by even more ugly green tile, Ms. Berry's voice just sounds like somebody humming, and I can't tell if any of the noise is coming from Bobby. For the first time ever, *the* Bobby Sanchez actually looked too scared to answer her. And I just know it's serious because nobody calls him by his real name. Nobody. Who knows what he did this time? But one thing I know is that I'd be in so much trouble if Dad ever had to leave his job to come deal with me in the middle of the school day. Even worse if it was Moms. The whole school would know what was up, and I'd be stuck doing everybody's chores for weeks! But I can't get the look on Bobby's face out of my head while I'm washing my hands. For the first time ever, he didn't have that mean smirk on his face he usually has when he's calling me some new dumb name he's made up. He sort of just sat there with his head down, ignoring the question. Like he didn't know how. But what do I know? Maybe he was scared of what would happen if he told the truth.

CHAPTER 11

"GET YOUR STUFF AND LET'S GO," AARON orders from the door of Mr. James's classroom with his eyes glued to his phone. "Mama told me to make sure to get you home 'in one piece,' and I gotta be somewhere." Whenever I can't walk home with Maria and Ms. Estelle, Moms pays Aaron five dollars to get me home safe, but he'd usually rather text his friends all the way home than watch me. Even though Maria told me this morning that Ms. Estelle was gonna pick her up early to go to the doctor, seeing Aaron in the hallway waiting for me makes me drag my backpack all the way out the door. "And pick yo' bag up off the floor. Mama's gon' get on me if I bring you home lookin' like you been rollin' around in some dirt." I throw it onto my back and groan loudly so he knows that even though I heard him, Notorious D.O.G. don't like being told what to do. Aaron walks off toward the front entrance so fast he probably doesn't even hear me.

There's three ways to get home from Booker T. You can go back down Locust Street, where everybody be out after school, you can go on the other side down Linden Street where don't nobody be, or you can cut through the Creighton Community Park. Mom and Dad said we're *never* allowed to do *that*.

For some reason, Aaron jets down the sidewalk to the left of the front doors toward Linden, even though that's not what me, Maria, and Ms. Estelle usually do. I try to tell him, but he already has on his headphones and is halfway down the parking lot sidewalk in his own world, trying to earn his five dollars as quick as possible.

From this side of Creighton Park, our hood,

we hear less people talking and more of the neighborhood sounds. Sirens scream over my head in between the ice cream truck's songs. Bass booms so loud from the cars that drive by that the sidewalk concrete shakes under my sneakers. Moms always says that's why old people are so hard of hearing. Listened to their jams too loudly when they were younger. *Jams* is Moms' word, not mine. Walking down this street so far behind Aaron makes me feel like I'm walking by myself, so I play a game where I concentrate real hard, trying to guess each song blaring from the car speakers, but they all just sound like shaky car doors with the same beat. I want Aaron to play it with me, but he's too far ahead of me to care.

THAT ONE WAS EASY, IT'S OLD–SCHOOL KANYE,
AND WHAT'S THIS SOUND LIKE? OH YEAH,
    BEYONCÉ.
"POP GOES THE WEASEL" STARTS LOW BUT GETS
    LOUD
AS THE BRIGHT YELLOW ICE CREAM TRUCK
    ROLLS AROUND.

AND THERE GOES THE SOUND OF THE GREEN
  LINE TRAIN!
BUT I'M USED TO IT NOW, OH SHOOT, LIL WAYNE!
AND IS DRAKE ON THAT ONE? THAT MUG SOUNDS
  HARD!
CAN'T WAIT TILL MY SONGS SHAKE EVERYBODY'S
  CAR!

Just past the funky Booker T. dumpster overflowing with leftover stale popcorn chicken, empty
milk cartons, and plastic fruit cups, Creighton
Community Park spreads across half of the back-
side of my school. It looks a lot different than
back when Dad stopped taking me there to play
on Saturdays after my haircut a few years ago. The
old sandbox is full of dandelions, the flower that
Moms calls weeds, and all the benches that used
to be a shiny green that matched the trees are now
a mix of rusty-looking oranges, reds, and yellows.
Where there used to be a tire swing, just a tire sits
on the ground covered in whatever trash is blowing around over there. The lump of blankets next
to some trash moves. *Whoa.* I look across the park

near the sandbox at another bench and see a pile of blankets that seems to be moving, too. *Wait.* I look back down the street and Aaron is already almost at the corner. *Did he see that happen, too?* There's an old sleeping bag under the tree near that corner surrounded by too many old grocery bags full of more and more bags, but nobody seems to be around.

"Simon, if you don't stop daydreamin' and come on! Short self always actin' like you can't keep up," Aaron yells back at me, suddenly noticing

I'm not close behind him, immediately annoyed. "Ain't nothin' to look at over there but bums and trash. We ain't goin' in there, so don't even think about it, man." I see my old favorite park to play at looking a lot like people live there now. *Bums and trash* doesn't sound right, but how do I say that to Aaron? He wouldn't care. I take another look across the park, wondering if I'll spot Sunny. Maybe he's hanging out with his friends or singing to himself somewhere with his stuff pushed under one of the benches Dad used to sit on while I made castles in the sandbox or watched the ants climb out of their little hills. "I said, *come on!*" I snap out of it and run up to meet Aaron at the corner, wishing he wouldn't boss me around like that. We never get to come on this side, and it's almost like we're in another city even though we're just around the corner from our house. Has it been this way the whole time?

CHAPTER 12

"WHERE Y'ALL BEEN AT?" MARKUS QUES--
tions me the minute me and Aaron walk in the
door, like he's our dad. His feet hang over the end
of the couch as usual, gaming control in his left
hand just the way he spent most of the summer.

"None of your business, Mark." Aaron never
likes being asked questions—by anybody. So when
he answers he doesn't *fully* answer, even for things
that aren't that serious. He also never calls Markus
by his full name.

"We went to the park," I say without thinking.
I still can't believe what I just saw—people lying

around so much trash and benches that looked like they'd been made into beds—and Aaron won't talk to me about it, so I have to tell Markus. He'll care about what I saw there. Or so I think.

"OoooWEE! Pop said we not supposed to go over there! I'm definitely finna tell on y'all."

"You know we ain't go to no park, Simon! Why you lyin' like that?" Aaron looks at me for the first time since picking me up from school. "And you better not, Mark. Unless you want me to tell Mama you was in here playing Fortnite before doin' your homework."

"Ain't no *real* homework in the first weeks, Ron Ron."

"I'm not lying, though. We did."

"We walked *by* the park. We ain't go *to* the park." I can't tell if Aaron is annoyed because I said we went to the park, because he had to bring me home before whatever he rather be doing, or because Markus called him the nickname he's been trying to shake since elementary school.

"Same thing." The way Aaron rolls his eyes and waves me off as he grabs his basketball makes me wonder why he didn't just tell me that's what he was on his way to do. Last year me, Maria, and C.J. would follow Aaron to the Locust Street ball court to cheer on the sidelines for whoever was winning. Aaron always looked like he hated it, though. Probably because his team was always losing. But he's a junior in high school now and I guess he can't have us around throwing off his game anymore.

Aaron pulls down his jeans, removing the layer of school clothes to reveal his bright red basketball shorts, and slips his feet into the new Jordans Dad bought him. We all wanted a pair as cool as Aaron's, but our parents said we can't get shoes that expensive until we're old enough to pay for them ourselves. Aaron didn't pay for his new Retro 11s, but working at Mr. Ray's sweeping up hair on the weekends means that he can. Enough money to pay Dad back for sneakers and have a little left over for snacks after the games he doesn't want us coming to.

"I'll be back right before Mama gets home. You better do your homework before I get back," Aaron says all serious as he ties his shoelaces three times over. He stands back up and stares into the mirror while he ties his red silk durag that matches his shorts tightly over the cornrows he just got braided at the top half of his head. He started getting only the sides and back shaved off after we saw *Black Panther* and he learned that all the girls in school liked Killmonger. He won't admit that's why, but we know.

"Okay," me and Markus answer at the same time, already doing what we want. Markus jerks and jumps, shooting and ducking things on the screen with his game control hands, while I pull my fist out of the cereal box to stuff a handful of Fruity-O's into my mouth just the way Moms told me she better not catch me doing. Crumbs fly from my mouth and hands, and I remind myself to clean up the evidence if I want to be allowed to get online with Maria and C.J. after dinner instead of being stuck on kitchen duty. I doubt Dad will come home early again the way he did a few days ago. I quickly eat the cereal that missed my mouth off the counter, scooping any dust that Moms might notice into my hands. Markus barely notices me move to the couch. I scoot closer to him to make sure he does.

"Dog, you're sitting *way* too close to me right now. You better back up before you get a whiff of what I just let out my butt." Markus always brings up farts when he wants to be left alone.

"Don't you want to know what I saw at the park?" Just then a cloud of funk that smells a lot like rotten eggs rises to my face, and I discover for once he isn't lying. But I need to talk about what I saw before Moms and Dad get home and think I really went into the park that Dad said we're not supposed to go to.

"Not really."

"There were people sleeping on the ground everywhere! Like they were full-on LIVING next to these piles of trash in the PARK! And some people were laying down under the benches with blankets and pillows like it was their bedroom! And there were bags and bags and bags everywhere! It was like the park had really become their house or something. And what happened to the—"

"They do live there," Markus says blankly

without taking his eyes off the screen, his body shooting back into the couch as he dodges his opponent in real life just like he was trying to do in the game. "You already knew that, Simon."

"In the park?" I guess the word *homeless*, to me, sounds like no home *of their own*. Like, maybe they just sleep at a different cousin's house each night. Which, I guess, feels better to imagine than having to sleep outside on the ground or a cold bench. Markus is right. I had seen this before, but something about it being in the park I used to play in made it more real.

"No, on Saturn. Where else, Simon? Isn't that where you're talking about?" Markus is over my questions, but I have like one million more to ask. I haven't been allowed to walk near Creighton Community Park since I was little, and my first time seeing it since then makes me feel like it's a whole new park. But old. And dirty. And full of people sleeping outside where everybody can see them. How do you sleep outside where everybody can see you? How about when it gets cold? Are you scared? What do you eat? How do you get food?

I don't know what I'd do without Moms' lasagna. Does Sunny live there, too? Is this where *all* the homeless people go at night? Markus leans away from me slightly and a loud rip sputters from under him. More rotten eggs (what do they eat in middle school?). Time to go. If I'm not going to play the game with him, he has nothing else to say to me.

FRiDAY

CHAPTER 13

FRIDAY'S HERE AND I CAN ALREADY FEEL how close Monday is from today. Dad doesn't even have to come knocking at the door the way he usually does. A whole hour before it's time to wake up, I lie in bed with the covers over my head, listening to Markus fight bedsheets in his sleep while DeShawn speaks to some character he's trying to defeat in his dream. It's like my body knows how close it all is.

I WISH THIS WAS A DREAM I COULD WAKE UP
FROM,

BUT MAN, IT'S A NIGHTMARE, AND I CAN'T RUN.

THIS PROJECT'S GONNA MAKE ME SOUND DUMB

SO, WORLDWIDE EMBARRASSMENT, HERE I COME!

The sun comes peeking through the window above my bed, reminding me that it's the weekend before the morning I hoped would never come. I lie as still as possible, hoping that if I never get out of bed or make any noise, maybe Friday will come and go without me. Maybe, magically, I'll get to skip another class of Mr. James pressuring me to be ready, and on Monday, somehow, I'll just know what to say. But the smell of bacon grease that comes floating under our bedroom door lets me know Dad isn't gon' be having any of that. I'm getting up whether I like it or not. So I brush my teeth and go downstairs.

"My maaaaaan." Dad's way of saying good morning during a week I'd rather skip altogether. "I'm whippin' up your favorites for breakfast. Come sit with your pops for a minute, son." I take a seat at the kitchen counter and stare at the bubbles growing around the edge of a pancake just before Dad flips it in the air the way he's been trying to teach me. "How'd you sleep?"

"Okay, I guess." I tossed and turned all night until DeShawn screamed *MAN, CHILL WITH ALL THAT!* from across the room. When it was time to go to bed, I laid down, rehearsing what I was going to say to my class for five minutes about a timely issue. I went to sleep picturing all the faces and thinking about what words would be okay to say, even if today isn't yet the real thing. Earlier in the week Mr. James said something about *practice* runs, and that sounded just as terrifying as when we do it on Monday. I feel like I stayed up all night trying to find the perfect words and think maybe I fell asleep only once, before Markus shook me out of a nightmare where I was at lunch with C.J. and Maria and went to take a bite of my pizza only to find out I had no mouth. "You're losin' it, man. Here," Markus whispered, handing me his phone and saying it'd help me go back to sleep. "Don't tell Dad."

"I know we're really close to the big day, and if it's getting harder to sleep, that's all right." Dad puts three pancakes, two pieces of bacon, and a scoop of eggs on my plate and leans over the counter, waiting for me to eat. The pancakes are fluffy and the eggs are cheesy—just the way I like them—but all I can do is look at it. Usually the smell makes my mouth water, but I don't feel even a little bit hungry.

"Um, thanks, Dad."

"How 'bout you go get dressed while you let this cool off, son. It'll be waiting for you when you get back." Secretly I hope Aaron wakes up and comes to steal it off my plate so I won't have to try to eat it. My stomach already feels all queasy about going to school: The idea of eating anything on top of that feeling makes it even worse. I know Dad is trying to make today a little easier because he sees me getting more and more nervous, but it isn't helping. He stares at me as I head back to my room to get dressed, which is even worse than when he reminded me today would be big, as if I didn't already have the nightmares to prove it. Back in the room behind the closed door, I get dressed slowly, trying to kill the time.

Mr. James says practicing in groups will help. But that don't seem any easier. It still means I have to talk in front of people in my class. It still means I could mess up and they could make fun of me. Just thinking about it makes me want to live in a cabin somewhere by myself like I hear about people doing in the movies. But there's no chance. Besides, I'd miss my friends.

"I know breakfast is your favorite thing to eat, so I packed yours up to take for lunch today. Plus, I had to put it away before your brothers got to it," Dad says, squeezing my shoulder, trying to get me to smile, laugh, something. I'm finally dressed and back in the living room, wishing he'd just act normal. I know he knows I still don't feel like eating, but he can't help but try to cheer me up. "You know your mama had to get to work early, but she told me to give you some love, too," he adds, patting the back of my neck.

"Thanks, Dad" is all I can squeeze out. It's mostly quiet walking up Locust Street, just the two of us, but it feels good even though I have nothing to say. At least I don't have to try so hard to pretend I feel like speaking. Dad always lets me be quiet when I don't have words. He never makes me feel like I gotta know what to say all the time.

SOMETIMES, SILENCE IS KEY.
I CAN BE IN MY HEAD WHERE MY
    THOUGHTS CAN BE FREE.
WHAT'S COOL IS I DON'T HAVE TO SPEAK.
I DON'T HAVE TO BE SHAKING, OR SWEATING,
    OR WEAK.

CUZ THE THOUGHTS IN MY HEAD ARE COMPLETE.
I KNOW JUST WHAT TO SAY, HOW TO MAKE IT
    SOUND SWEET.
NOBODY CAN HEAR IT BUT ME.
YEAH, NOBODY CAN HEAR IT BUT ME.

As I turn into the parking lot, my heart starts thumping too hard against my chest. It gets so loud I don't hear Dad saying my name until he turns to kneel down in front of me at the bottom of the front steps.

"Simon, my man. Rhymin' Simon. BIG—"

"I get it, Dad." Dad always tries hyping me up for things by thinking of every cool version of my name. But most of the time it just sounds silly and makes me laugh. It just makes him sound like an old man. Nothing can really make me laugh right now anyway.

"What's that name you got everybody callin' you now?"

"Notorious D.O.G."

"Do you know what that word means?" The truth is I don't, really. I just know all the famous rappers have names that make them sound important or special, and last year C.J.'s dad dressed him up for Halloween as one of his favorites: Notorious B.I.G., an old rapper from New York City who everybody knew about before we were born. C.J. looked just like what I'd seen in the pictures with his leather jacket, gold chain, and old-man hat turned to the side. And C.J. was big like him, too. He looked like somebody nobody would mess with, and that night at the neighborhood Halloween party, nobody did. I knew I needed a name like that. And I knew a lot of people were scared of dogs, so.

"Somebody important?" I finally say back.

"It means somebody that everybody knows. And it *usually* means that everybody knows them for something they did. No matter what happens today or Monday, people are gon' know you for something good you did, son. First because you got up there and used that voice of yours. Second, because you always doin' good even when you feel scared or like you might mess up." Dad's fist rises into the air in front of our chests to dap me up before he moves out of the way so I can walk up the steps to go inside. Just as Ms. Berry waves hello to Dad, Bobby comes running up the sidewalk from the community park side of the building that me and Aaron walked past yesterday after school. Bobby is empty-handed.

Moms and Dad would never let me come to school with no backpack, but I guess Bobby follows his own rules even outside of school.

"Good morning, Mr. Sanchez. Glad to see you on time. Unprepared," the principal says, looking him up and down like she's confused, "but on time. That's something, I guess." Bobby sort of keeps his head down as he rushes to get in the door before I do, only looking over at me for a second. He's breathing all hard and sweating so much his extra-long white tee and Pistons shorts are already sticking to his body. I wonder how many pairs of Pistons shorts in this same color does Bobby have? And white tees? It can't be that many if the one he's wearing isn't even white anymore. School hasn't even started for the day yet and Bobby looks like he's been playing football all morning. But Creighton Park don't have a football field and Bobby Sanchez don't play no football. I look to see where Victor and Justin are, thinking maybe it's because they've all already picked on a fourth grader before the first bell has even rung, but Bobby's by himself for once.

"Move," he says under his breath, his shoes flapping loosely against his feet. As rough as he looks today, I'm surprised he didn't even put on some decent sneakers. I feel like Bobby could be the one getting picked on today with the way he looks.

"SIMON!" Maria yells my name from the doorway of Mr. James's class. I walk past her and go straight to my seat, keeping my head low, wishing everybody would stop making such a big deal about everything. She follows me and plops down at her desk, turning around to stare at me while I unpack my backpack.

"Oh, so you just gonna ignore me, Simon? That's all right, I missed you, too," she says, laughing at my attitude. "Today's gonna be so fun! It's gonna be like we're in a play...but with presentations."

"That don't even make sense, Ri-Ri. You prolly the only one who thinks that sounds like fun."

"Yes it does! Who says you can't be anybody you want while you practice? Maybe you wouldn't be so scared if you did it in *character*."

LIGHTS, CAMERA, ACTION!
SIGNING AUTOGRAPHS WITH THE
    CAMERAS FLASHIN',
WHERE'S MY AWARD FOR THIS AWESOME ACTIN'?

Maria's idea doesn't sound that crazy when I think about it for a second, but then I start feeling real stressed. Practicing what I'm gonna say on Monday *and* pretending to be somebody else while I do it?! This is getting out of control.

"I hope Mr. James just forgets all about it."

"You silly, Simon. It's not gonna be that bad. Plus! We could be partners with Lil Kenny! You know he don't care. And I'll be nice!" The idea of practicing with Maria feels comforting, and I hadn't thought about picking my own group to practice with, but I still don't wanna do it.

Mr. James closes the door seconds after the bell rings. "Good morning, scholars! It's Friday, so you know what time it is," he says, pausing and taking a slow look around the room. *Gurgle.* I try to ignore the loud swishy feeling that rises in my stomach as I think about what he's gonna say next, but it only gets worse. "Practice rounds of oral presentations! I'm sure you're all excited to see what your classmates got so far. Y'all ready or what?"

It's quieter than it was on the first day when he said good morning to us for the first time. Why would anybody be ready for this? Talking to each other about *timely* stuff? *Gurgle.* Pretending like it's the real thing? *Gurgle.* I touch my stomach, trying to get it to chill, but there's no real chill in sight.

"Well, ready or not, let's do this." Mr. James turns to a plastic cup on his desk full of what looks like used-up Popsicles. I mean, there's no red juice left on them, but I know they're the same sticks that be inside the Firecracker freezy pops me, Maria, and C.J. ate all summer. He turns back around and stands there for a second while it feels like nobody in the room is breathing. "We gon' break y'all into groups. Random groups." *Come on, man!* The whole class lets out a groan while we all look around, nervous about who we'll have to work with. I thought today couldn't get any worse. Surprise.

Mr. James starts pulling Popsicle sticks with each of our names written on them out of the cup, one by one, calling each of us to get in groups of three, and I slowly watch the only people I feel okay around get picked for groups I'm not in. First Maria gets picked. Then Lil Kenny. And finally me.

"Simon Barnes... Russell Taylor... Bobby Sanchez."

Help.

Somebody help me. Please don't make me have to use my legs to walk over there where Bobby is.

Maria turns around from the corner she's now sitting in with her group, leans over the back of her chair, and smiles so big her teeth look bigger than her whole face. I can't help but give her the angriest look I can give my best friend so she'll turn back around. Somehow, I float to the back of the room where Bobby and Russell are already sitting, looking back to see Mr. James's eyeballs following me. I notice a lot more eyeballs than his watching me walk back there, eyeballs of people who'd know better than to put me with Bobby.

Standing in front of Bobby, I stare down at the flash cards in my hands and notice my hands shaking so hard I wonder how my body can feel so cold when it's still summer outside.

MR. JAMES DON'T LIKE ME...HE <u>HATES</u> ME PROBLY.

 WHY <u>ELSE</u> WOULD HE HAVE ME PRACTICE WITH BOBBY?

DON'T HE KNOW THAT ME AND SANCHEZ ARE
    NOT COOL?
OUT OF EVERYONE AT SCHOOL, I GET PUT WITH
    THIS FOOL?!

UGH! I SWEAR TO YOU, IT'S SOMETHIN' I DON'T
    CARE TO DO.
IT'S ABSOLUTELY TERRIBLE, AND SUPER
    UNBEARABLE.
WORST GROUP EVER! WORST WEEK EVER!
DO I THINK THIS WILL WORK? NO, NOPE, NAH,
    NEVER!

"All right, everybody. We've got ten minutes. You each get three minutes to try out with your group what you're thinking about doing, and you can use the last minute to tell each other what y'all think. You can switch the person who's presenting when you hear the *ding* on the timer. Have fun and be nice to the people in your group, all right?" He starts the timer, puts it down on his desk, and leans back. I'm beginning to think Mr. James loves seeing us all freak out.

"You go first, Barnes," Bobby orders, staring at

me from the seat he hasn't even moved from, his back leaning against the wall and his legs spread out like he's chilling at home on the couch. "Show us what you got." I shuffle back and forth on my feet. The timer is ticking, so I look down at my flash cards and try to say something.

"Homelessness," I whisper, clearing my throat and pulling at the collar of my favorite polo Moms bought me last year. I laid it out last night cuz I always wear it when I need to feel okay. Nobody knows that, though. I say the word again, hoping the rest of the words will come. "Homelessness."

"AND?" Russell blurts out. Bobby doesn't even try to keep his snickering under his breath. He laughs out loud. I shuffle the flash cards in my hand and then remember I put them in order for a reason. I need them to remember what to say. Panicking, I try finding the first card again.

"Um...homelessness," I say a third time, trying to stall. *Oh no. OH NO.*

"*AY YO! MR. JAMES! BARNES AIN'T SAYIN' NOTHIN'!*" Bobby screams out, leading the whole class to turn toward us and laugh at me this time.

My hands freeze as I look up to see Bobby staring back at me. Leaning forward in his desk, he grabs the edge of it, and Russell joins him in staring me down. Except Bobby doesn't say anything else. He just starts looking more annoyed than usual. Like he's tired of me saying *that* word and wishes I would just move on or something. Which confuses me. Bobby normally acts like he could watch me suffer forever.

Gurgle. Guuuuurgle. Suddenly I can taste last night's spaghetti rising up in my belly like it needs to go back where it came from—which is outside

my body. *GURGLE.* Then I can actually feel the noodles filling my mouth. Dropping the flash cards I wrote all over last night trying to be prepared for today, I run to the door, flinging it open, and speed all the way down the hallway past Ms. Berry's office. Ms. Berry don't like kids running in the hallway, but this is an emergency.

Splash! Red sauce and half-chewed spaghetti noodles cover the floor just inside the boys' bathroom and keep coming out of me too fast for me to get to a toilet. Moms is right. I eat waaay too fast. How did unchewed noodles make it in there? *Oh no.* Just when I thought I was in here by myself and was glad no one would see, a toilet flushes and the stall lock unlatches. Justin steps out to wash his hands but freezes in front of the sink when he notices me and stares. Not seeing Bobby's sidekicks with him this morning made me think they hadn't come to school today, but I was wrong.

"Yikes, man."

CHAPTER 14

NOTORIOUS D.O.G. MIGHT BE THE FIRST fifth grader in history at Booker T. to run out of class in the middle of a presentation to puke. This morning when Dad told me being notorious meant to be known for something I did, I didn't know it was gonna be this. I didn't know it'd be because I'd lose my words in front of my small group right before losing last night's dinner on the floor of the bathroom. Dad picks me up from the nurse's office, shaking his head, laughing. He can't even pretend to be serious about this.

"It's not funny."

"It's not? Now you can be known as the Notorious G.A.G. Come on! So catchy," he says, slinging my backpack over his left shoulder and pushing me out the door with his free hand. "You probably set a new school record, son." I don't feel like talking. All morning everyone either laughed at me or smiled in my face like everything was so funny, but my worst nightmare has finally come true and even Dad got jokes. At least it's Friday and Dad hadn't left for work yet. At least he could come when they called him. At least he isn't mad at me for bombing the first try at my first fifth-grade assignment.

"Rhymin' Simon! Whatchu doin' home from school so early, big man?" Sunny pauses to look at his wrist to check the time on a watch he isn't wearing. "Time just be goin' by so fast these days, can't tell my up from down. My left from right. My morning from night! Look at that, my boy. Your rhymes are startin' to rub off on me."

"How you doin', Sunny?" Dad says back to him so I don't have to.

"Oh, I'm all right, man," Sunny says, still staring at me, then pointing. "But what's wrong with the boy? Look like somethin' wrong wit' him. He don't look too good."

"Rough morning, Sunny. We'll catch you later." Dad squeezes my shoulder and leads me up the apartment building stairs.

Five hours later Dad wakes me up with a knock on my door. He looks down at the trash can he moved from the bathroom into my room next to my bed, and then looks back at me like he's surprised.

"Brought you some ginger ale. And some crackers for that queasy stomach." Drinking soda is all of a sudden okay with adults when something's wrong with your stomach. As long as it's nasty ginger ale. For Dad and Moms, ginger ale fixes everything.

"I don't need no crackers, Dad. I'm not even sick."

"Oh really? So people just be throwin' up at school and goin' about their business all the time, huh? What you gonna tell me next, that you were just clearing your throat?" Dad flashes a smile.

"I'm serious, Dad. I'm okay."

"What was it, then, Si?"

"I—I—I was...I was scared."

"Ah. But we talked about this! You don't have anything to be sc—"

"That's not true! Everybody keeps acting like everything is so easy. Nobody knows how I feel. Nobody understands." I drop my head down and hear Dad let out a deep sigh. All of a sudden he's sitting on the bed next to me. But he doesn't say anything for a few minutes.

"My bad, son. I guess I just wanted you to not feel like that. Maybe I made too big a deal about trying to make you not feel scared when I should have tried to help you feel brave."

"Brave?"

"Yeah. Being brave don't mean you not scared or afraid. It means you feel those things but you do it anyway. There's a lot of things that are scary. If we all waited till we didn't feel scared, we'd never do anything, son. I was scared when me and your uncle got on that stage way back then."

"Really?"

"Yeah, man. Peed on myself a little bit when I

stepped under those spotlights and really looked out into the audience, seein' everybody lookin' up at me." What!

"You're just saying that to make me feel better."

"Nah, son. Your granny had a FIT when she saw that stain in my pants when she was doin' the laundry! Lectured me like I was a little kid about making sure I went to the bathroom before going to bed, for WEEKS after that." The thought of Grandma Lucille telling Dad to make sure he peed before bed when he was a teenager makes me laugh till ginger ale comes squirting out my nose.

"Aye, chill, chill, chill. I ain't tell you all that so you can clown your dad, okay? But, you see, we're even now." I wipe my nose on my sleeve and we get quiet for a long time.

"Dad?"

"Yeah, son?"

"Can we go back to the shelter...please?"

"Didn't you already—"

"Please?"

"All right, son. But first, drink some more of that ginger ale."

☆ ☆ ☆

This time Miss Wanda looks surprised to see me and Dad back at Creighton Park Community Outreach. On a Friday after school, everything feels different. Walking in, we notice a huge line out the door and around the block, and I don't find a lot of the faces I saw earlier in the week. Not only are there tons of people, but a lot of them are teenagers and little kids, too. A weird smell that I remember from my visits before is much stronger. I follow behind Dad to the dining hall, searching for Sunny through all the people waiting to get something to eat.

"It's this many homeless people in Creighton Park, Dad?" I have to keep my mouth from hanging open, and Moms is always telling me it's rude to stare.

"Yeah, son."

"I don't think Sunny's here, Dad."

"That's who you came to see?"

"Yeah, Dad. Where is he?" I ask, suddenly feeling embarrassed as I realize I don't know where Sunny sleeps every night.

"Well, that's hard to say. Even though this place feeds a lot of people in need in our community, they still run out of food, and they don't have a lot of space for people to stay." I notice Miss Wanda has put on an apron and gloves to help serve and is standing near the front of the food line as we walk by. "There's a lot goin' on here today, Simon. Sunny's luck probably ran out today."

"Miss Wanda, is Mr. Sunny here?"

"Ain't seen him today yet, baby." I know Miss Wanda doesn't know me, so I let her call me that even though the Notorious D.O.G. ain't no baby. On the way out the door I get an idea.

"Dad?"

"Yeah, Si?"

"Can we go to the corner store?" Dad looks down at me like he wants to tell me no because of my queasy stomach or because him and Moms don't think we need to be eating *all that junk*.

"Please? It's not for me, Dad."

CHAPTER 15

OUTSIDE OF CHICAGO CORNER MY STOM--
ach grumbles at the smell of the catfish sandwich
and fries coming from the box I'm holding in my
hand, while I try to think of a way to get Dad to
walk me to the park. We see Sunny outside of our
apartment building all the time, but I had a feeling
he wouldn't be there this time. If there isn't space
for him at the shelter, where else would he go for
something to eat?

"Dad?"

"Yeah, Simon?" Dad says, looking like he's over
me asking for stuff today.

"Um…can we go to the park?" Especially stuff I already know we aren't allowed to do.

"Now, Simon, you know I don't like y'all goin' in there."

"But what if Sunny's there, Dad? I have to give this to him. What if he's really hungry?" Dad looks around and then up at the sky for a minute before looking back down at me. I make sure I have on my best *pretty please* face. Dad has a soft spot for my sad face. He doesn't say it out loud, but I know that between me and my brothers, the Notorious D.O.G. is his favorite.

"All right, Si," he says, kneeling in front of me for a second. "But you stay right next to me and don't talk to nobody we don't know, got it?"

"Okay, Dad."

Walking into the park is a lot different than walking past it. Now I know for sure it isn't the park that me and C.J. used to play at on Saturdays. It stinks real bad and there's garbage everywhere, even though there's trash cans. We walk halfway down the block, back down Loving toward the homeless shelter again, and turn onto a sidewalk that goes all the way through the park. I stay close next to Dad while I look at all the tall trees on both sides of the long sidewalk, with plastic bags piled at the bottoms of all their trunks. Trash bags full of clothes and other weird things instead of trash. I move closer to Dad when I notice people staring at us from behind some of the benches, talking to themselves. A few are going through the overflowing trash cans, looking for food. I've never seen Sunny around this park or even going through a trash can. The thought of him doing that makes me upset. I don't know if we'll find him here, and that makes the feeling even worse.

"Two more minutes and we're out of here, Simon."

"Visitors! I ain't had visitors in years! You should have called first. I would have baked a cake and fried up some wings!" Sunny's voice booms from a bench close to Linden. The bench that isn't too far from where I was standing and staring into the park just a few days ago before Aaron noticed I was far behind. "Can I get you a glass of water? Pop for the kiddo?"

IS SUNNY BEING FUNNY TRYNA GIVE US A DRINK?
YEAH, HE'S PROBLY JOKING, WELL, AT LEAST, I
   THINK.
HE SAID IT WITH A SMILE, AND HE GAVE US A
   WINK.
DOES HE HAVE SOME ICED TEA, OR LEMONADE
   THAT'S PINK?

"That's okay, Sunny. I brought *you* something," I say, looking up at Dad. He nods, giving me the signal that it's okay to step closer to Sunny. *Go 'head*, he mouths.

"My maaan," Sunny says back, sounding just like Dad. "Whatchu got there?" I feel funny getting this close to Sunny outside the shelter, but he sort of reminds me of Grandpa John, his voice always sounding so warm. Sunny smells like so many things, but I don't know what. Whatever it is, it smells like it's been on him for too many days. Grandma Lucille would never approve. He's been sweeping up leaves and trash on our block since I was little and he always has a smile on his face, but not so much this time. I've even seen him dancing around on the sidewalk with whichever broomstick he's using like he was at a party with somebody, having the best time. Sometimes he even has on a dressy suit jacket that he found somewhere, making it look even more like the sidewalk is the fanciest party ever and he's the special guest.

This time he looks different, though. Like the way Moms looks when she works the night shift. But times twenty. Or like when Dad says he's disappointed in something me and my brothers did. But times, like, one hundred. Sunny hums to himself and shuffles around on the bench a little bit while I take the box out of the plastic bag.

"I couldn't find you at the shelter. Are you hungry?" It feels like a silly question, but I don't know what else to say.

"I guess I could eat," he says, looking over my head at my dad. He scratches at his neck where I see his collarbone poking out until he covers it back up. I hand him the box. My stomach grumbles a little, smelling the catfish and crinkle fries. I laugh to myself, hearing Moms telling us how her catfish is way better than anything we could get at the store. "Thank you, kiddo," Sunny says with a little water in his eyes. He starts doing a little bop, bouncing his shoulders and then swaying back and forth in his seat while chewing his first bite. On the second bite, he shoots up out of his seat, doing some footwork I've seen both Dad and Grandpa John do when they're happy.

"What you know about that, young'un? You don't know nothin' about that good ol' two-step, my boy! This is before your time! I ain't had catfish in forever! What they put in this seasoning?" Sunny keeps dancing around his bench, taking bites into the bread and fried fish like we're not even there. Maria dances when she's eating, too. I smile extra hard, knowing we made Sunny happy enough to do the eating dance. He pauses from the sandwich to move on to the fries, stuffing a handful into his mouth at a time, not caring about the grease spreading all around his mouth the way crumbs get on my face eating Fruity-O's. I wait a second for him to take a break.

"Can I come talk to you some more tomorrow, Sunny?"

"*Mi casa es su casa*, my boy," he jokes with a new mouthful of fried fish and white bread, one arm opened across the bench. "You know where to find me next time. I just gotta make it through the night. Thanks for the grub, big man."

SATURDAY

CHAPTER 16

"SO I TOLD 'EM...I TOLD 'EM I AIN'T getting onstage without my special microphone! I told 'em they gon' have to get another lead singer if they can't find it." Sunny high-fives one of his friends.

"I know that's right!" At one in the afternoon, Sunny has a whole audience of homeless friends in the dining hall of Creighton Park Community Outreach surrounding him for story time. Everybody's leaning in to listen to him talk about his younger days as the lead singer of a blues band.

"So what they do?" one lady asks, staring at Sunny like his story was her favorite movie ever.

"They found them another lead singer!"

Sunny's whole table busts out laughing as crumbs of food fly through all the empty spaces where their teeth used to be. From across the room me, C.J., and Maria walk toward his table while he catches his breath. The sound of Sunny's wheezing after laughing at his own stories is funnier than the stories. I feel happy just seeing Sunny be Sunny again.

"Moral of the story: Keep yo' microphone in yo' pocket at ALL times!" Sunny is the life of the party, and it's strange hearing him talk about his old life. It makes me even more curious. "So you could be...How that song go? *Irreplaceable...*," Sunny sings, trying to use the words of that Beyoncé song I heard playing the other day to finish telling his story. I walk toward him with Maria by my side while C.J. wanders around, dapping people up at different tables like everybody is now his friend after meeting some of them only once before. Whatever his dad told him about staying away from someone who is homeless seems to be melting away.

Maria's never been to the shelter with me, so she stays close, walking with her left arm linked into my right. It feels kind of good to be showing another best friend the place Dad showed me just a few days ago. A place I didn't even know was so close to us, down the street from my house, where so many people in our neighborhood have to eat because they don't have money to get food from anywhere else.

"Rhymin' Simon! You're back!"

"Hi, Sunny," I say, feeling proud that he's so happy to see me.

"*Maria, Mariaaaaaa,*" he sings, swaying and two-stepping toward Maria. She smiles back at him but looks around for a minute at everyone else, squeezing my arm tighter. Usually I'm the one who gets nervous, but I guess even though Sunny isn't new, everyone else is too many strangers for her at once. Maybe how Ms. Estelle feels about people who are homeless has rubbed off on Maria a little.

"Hi, Mr. Sunny," Maria finally squeezes out while using her pointer finger to push her glasses higher up on her nose. Today the frames are lime green.

"I like those glasses, Miss Maria," Sunny says back to her softly. I can tell he's trying to make her feel comfortable being somewhere she's never been before.

"Bruh, everybody in here LOVES me," C.J. yells to us across the dining hall, already sitting squeezed all cozy in between some of Sunny's friends at a table where they're playing chess. I turn toward C.J., making sure he sees me rolling my eyes at him, even though I've always thought it was so cool how C.J. makes people love him everywhere he goes. Maria lets go of my arm and runs over to him to get in on the action. I turn back around and sit down across from Sunny. Maria will make sure C.J. doesn't do anything he isn't supposed to while we wait for Ms. Estelle to pick us up in an hour.

"Came to tell me about how that new teacher of yours done gave you a ONE HUNNEDT on that project, didn't you? I just know your whole class gave you a round of applause!" Sunny's smiling way too hard for me to tell him the truth right away. He's in too much of a good mood for me to tell him I've already freaked out and the actual big day still hasn't come yet.

"Um...something like that...err...the whole class made...a lot of noise when I was done."

"That's my guy!" Sunny raises his hand in the air to high-five me, and the rest of the truth splurts out just like my guts did all over the bathroom floor yesterday afternoon.

"I don't know what I got on my project, Sunny. I don't really present until Monday, but I ran out of the room before I could even say anything for real yesterday when we were practicing in our groups. Everybody...everybody was laughing at me before I could even get my words out. One of my partners made fun of me and then everybody was looking at our group and laughing. I don't know what happened. But it was like everything

just disappeared out of my head like a magic trick."
I feel Sunny's eyes on me even though my head's
down as I try to tell him how I lost my voice in
front of the whole class. That I couldn't do it even
though I knew what I was supposed to present was
important.

I LET SUNNY DOWN YESTERDAY, AND I CAN
    FEEL IT.
I KNOW HE BELIEVED I WOULD ABSOLUTELY
    KILL IT!
INSTEAD, SCAREDY SIMON MESSED UP AND
    BLEW IT.

NOW THE WHOLE HOMELESS SHELTER'S GONNA
    KNOW I LOOKED STUPID.

I WISH I COULD CRAWL AWAY FROM THIS
    CONVERSATION

LIKE I WISH I COULD WALK AWAY FROM MY
    PRESENTATION.
I WISH I COULD RUN, BUT THE DAMAGE IS DONE.
GOTTA BE A BIG DOG AND ACCEPT WHAT'S TO
    COME.
WOOF WOOF

"Oh. You didn't say nothin' at all?"

"Well…I did say…something." I don't want to tell him the word. I don't know if he calls himself what we call him.

"And what is that?" he asks, scratching the top of his head, making me wonder what his hair used to look like before he got old.

"Um…um…"

"Go on, spit it out, son. You ain't in class now. I ain't nobody." I want to tell Sunny that isn't true. I want to tell him that's why I've been feeling like I'm failing at this project. Sunny is somebody.

"Homelessness."

"What's that, now?" He leans in, sticking a finger in one ear and wiggling it like he's clearing out wax. "Speak up."

"I said *homelessness*." Saying the word so loud in front of Sunny makes me want to hide under the table. He's old like Grandma Lucille, who has a house on the South Side. I like going to Grandma Lucille's house because she always has all kinds of food in her fridge and something baking in the oven when we come over. And she has a room in her house with a bed made up just for me and my brothers to stay the night when we feel like it. She has a car and a dog named Lucky, too. I thought that was what all old people had. *Homeless* doesn't sound like the right word to use for Sunny. Saying it in front of him makes me feel like I'm calling him a rude name. Like something Bobby might call me.

"Now, that wasn't so hard, was it?" is all Sunny says at first.

"It was," I whisper.

"I don't know why, my boy. That's what the topic is, ain't it? And that's what I deal with every day. I ain't ashamed of it, son. And it ain't a bad word," he says as if he just read my mind. "I know why you're here, Simon. And you know what? I'm glad about it."

I finally lift up my head, looking at him for the first time in the past few minutes.

"All these times y'all came to see me this week and all those questions you been asking make me feel real good inside. Like people really care about me. It's nice knowing somebody cares about your story."

Sunny smiles hard with all his teeth, and I sit there not knowing what to say. All this time I've been scared to say the truth about Sunny, and having someone care about his story is what's making him feel so happy.

"You be eatin' that food over there, Mr. Sunny?" Maria asks, plopping back down at our table, with C.J. coming to sit down right behind her. She doesn't look so nervous about being here anymore, and that means Sunny will see how much she can talk. I didn't even hear them coming, and her voice snapped me out of it. "If my 'buela Estelle was here, she'd say it needs a lot more sazón! And where is the—"

"Maria!" I growl, elbowing her in her side before she can say anything else. She's already found time to hang with C.J.'s table and inspect the food being served. The table shakes and doesn't stop for a few minutes. Me and Maria think it's C.J. getting comfortable in his seat, but when we look up it's Sunny. Tears falling down his face, laughing at us hard. It seems like a long time before he finally stops and wipes his face.

"Y'all remind me of my Patti," he says, still breathing loudly after laughing so hard at us.

"Who's that?" C.J. asks.

"My wife," he tells us, smiling and looking down at his left hand, rubbing on one of his fingers. The same finger my mom and dad wear their wedding rings. "Couldn't nobody stop her from speaking her mind. She said what she had to say and asked whatever she felt like asking, but I couldn't ever get her on that stage with me no matter what I tried. We met when we was kids. Just like y'all. Getting in all kinds of trouble all over Creighton Park back when it was still safe to play by ourselves out there and kids could walk home from school by themselves. One day I watched her climb up a tree to rescue her old cat, Paw Paw, and the rest was history. I ain't seen a girl climb a tree like that before. I ain't never climbed a tree before and there she was, all the way up in a tree like it wasn't nothing. I didn't leave her side after that."

Old people are always talking about history, but I look at C.J. and Maria and can tell, just like me, they're surprised to hear Sunny's. When Dad brought me to the shelter the first time to serve, I just thought maybe I'd ask Sunny about what it's like not having a house. I never really thought to ask him about his family and the things he likes. It's strange thinking maybe he had all the things I have now and still ended up here. Somehow. It's even more strange to think of Sunny ever being little like me.

"That's right. I was eleven years old once. Hard to believe, right? I know you been thinking about climbin' them trees outside. Don't do it!" Sunny got jokes, raising his hands up in front of us while his eyes get all big like he's really trying to stop us.

"I've never seen anybody climb a tree in Creighton Park," C.J. says, like it's the craziest thing he's ever heard.

"Yeah," Maria adds. "I'd be grounded till I was sixty-three years old!"

"Well, this city ain't what it used to be. Can't play the same way around here," Sunny says, getting all serious, which makes the three of us get super quiet.

"Did you have to do presentations in front of your class when you were in the fifth grade, Sunny?" I know it's time for me to ask Sunny some real questions. Joking is fun and all. But something reminds me I don't have a lot of time. Who knows where Sunny might be tonight or the next day?

"Of course, man. I wasn't too much of a good student, though. Except for in music class. Me, I knew I wanted to be an artist." Sunny's long, spacey yellow teeth shine in the light when he says that. This must be what Moms be talkin' about when she tries to tell me what'll happen to my teeth if I don't brush *and* floss twice a day.

"All the other boys wanted to be engineers and doctors and mechanics like their pops told them they should, but not me. All I wanted to do was *sang*," Sunny continues, looking out across the dining hall like he's daydreaming right in front of us.

"You sing so nice, Mr. Sunny. My mama look like her head hurts when I sing in the house." We all laugh, thinking about Maria's mom having to plug her ears at Maria's voice.

"Thank you, little sis. Too bad sangin' ain't pay my bills. I learned that the hard way when I got older. And since I ain't pay enough attention in school, there was less for me to do."

"So what'd you do?" Everybody's into this. Even C.J.

"I got me a job! Walked down there to Booker T. and put in an application to clean them toilets and mop them floors back at my old elementary school! Figured I ain't know a lot but I knew my way around *that* place." *Whaaaat?*

All three of us sit there with our mouths hanging open, not believing what we just heard, so Maria makes sure we didn't imagine it.

"*YOOOU* WENT TO BOOKER T.?! That's crazy, Mr. Sunny. 'Buela is always talking about how different school was for her as a little niña in Puerto Rico and how grateful we should be. I told her all the tables in the cafeteria is broken and she said everything looks so new and pretty. I'm gonna tell her Booker T. has been open for hundreds and HUNDREDS of years!"

"Whoa whoa whoa," Sunny says, chuckling and raising his hands up for Maria to slow down. "I ain't that old, baby girl." Sunny's hands send a little breeze over to our side of the table that reminds me of how he smelled when I handed him the box of food yesterday in the park. It kind of smelled like something that was in the air yesterday morning walking into school just before everything went sideways. Maybe I'm imagining it. Sunny wasn't even around.

"So you gave up your dream to be a singer?" I have to know. How did Sunny get here? If he did the right thing by getting a job, how is he sitting in the shelter with us right now?

"Never. Crazy part about being a janitor is that nobody ever really talks to you. It got lonely sometimes, but I sang through those halls every day until it was time to clock out. I ain't have no stage to get on or even know the first thing about how to be a singer in the world, but I did what I could. That school had the best acoustics, man," he says, shaking his head like what he's telling us is sad.

"What about what you were telling everybody earlier?"

"Oh, that band I used to sing wit'? Can't sing to yourself too long before somebody else who likes music finds you. Before I knew it I was jamming with the other folk who did thangs around the school after we got off work. I had a good thing goin' on for a while."

"So then what happened, Sunny?" C.J. asks.

"What you mean, my boy?"

"What happened to you, if you had a job?" Leave it up to C.J. to be rude. I give him a look and he raises his hands the way you do when you tell somebody you don't know something. I guess I do want to know.

"Budget cuts. School got a new principal and all of a sudden all the jobs they said wasn't important started getting cut. Back then I ain't know that much about money, so it got real hard after that, kiddo. Real hard." Sunny drifts off the same way he did the first day I got to hang out with him here. I don't like how sad he looks, but this time I feel kind of happy to know more about him. "Sang for a while out here, ya know. I had a real good voice and people paid money to see me, here and there. Learned I could use it to help take care of me and Patti for a while. It was real hard, but all I knew was that it felt good when I was singin'. All them people comin' out to hear me made me feel like something."

"Did you ever get scared?" Maria sneaks a quick look at me before looking back at him.

"All the time, lil sis." Then he looks back at me. "But I had to remember that, besides my gal Patti, all I had was my voice at the end of the day. Nobody else has this voice. It's what makes me *me*."

"I know what you mean," I say, almost whispering. I'm talking to Sunny but keep my eyes on the table. "I be getting nervous sometimes when this kid Bobby at school tries to mess with me. A-a-and like when I gotta do stuff in front of the whole class…but when I'm rhyming…I don't feel so scared or so little anymore. I feel good about being me."

"Then you should keep doing it, my boy. Do it all the time till you feel that way about yourself *all the time*." I try to think about what Sunny is saying. About how I can use my skills to help me really feel like the Notorious D.O.G. Sunny never stopped singing, and even though a lot of bad stuff has happened in his life he's still Sunny.

"Now you know I ain't forget about that promise you made me, right?" Sunny says. I smile back at Sunny even though I feel a little *gurgle* coming on deep down in my belly.

"Wanna tell me about what happened yesterday, again?" Then Sunny starts clapping slow like he's giving me a beat. Maria sways to it while C.J. becomes my hype man, moving his hands around to the beat in the air, doing his best Notorious B.I.G. impression the way his dad taught him.

UHN...UHN...YEAH...LET'S GO...
I AIN'T REALLY PLAN FOR ANY OF
   THIS TO HAPPEN
BUT I MADE A PROMISE, I'D LET YOU HEAR ME
   RAPPIN'.
USUALLY I DO THIS AT THE CRIB IN FRONT OF
   FAMILY,
NOT IN FRONT OF PEOPLE, SO YOU GOTTA
   UNDERSTAND ME...

WHEN I SAY I'M NERVOUS, AND Y'ALL CAN PROBLY
    HEAR IT.
VOICE IS KINDA SHAKY, SUPER BASIC LYRICS.
BUT IT'S GETTING BETTER AS I GO, THIS I KNOW,
CUZ I CAN SEE THE WAY Y'ALL ARE ROCKIN' TO
    MY FLOW.

ALL THANKS TO SUNNY, I'M RAPPIN' OUT IN
    PUBLIC.
NOW WHEN I'M AT SCHOOL TALKIN', I CAN CRUSH
    IT!
SO LOUD AND FREE, I'M SO PROUD OF ME,
NOT SIMON, BUT NOTORIOUS D.O.G.
WOOF WOOF!

CHAPTER 17

"ALL HANDS OUT, PLEASE," MS. ESTELLE demands once we walk out of the shelter. Globs of hand sanitizer squirt from the small bottle that's always clipped to her purse. "And make sure you rub it in real good. You're not comin' en la casa with all those outside germs." Me, C.J., and Maria make sure the gooey stuff touches every corner of our hands long enough for us to smell like rubbing alcohol. Which basically means we all smell like Grandma Lucille's medicine cabinet. Ms. Estelle checks all of our fingers even though you wouldn't really be able to see germs if they were still there.

"You need to clip those nails, niña," she tells Maria before we walk back toward our apartments.

Dad and Moms went to run errands this morning and left all three of us with Ms. Estelle for most of the day, so we head to Maria's to eat. My stomach grumbles at the thought of what we'll eat, while I'm still hype off of my first real rap performance outside of the house. It gets louder as we get closer to their building, letting me know I'm *crazy* hungry. Rappin' is hard work!

That night we have rice and beans, stewed chicken, and tostones, which look like light green bananas that somebody smashed into the table with their fist. If Moms saw me eating she'd be big mad at my manners for shoving so much food into my face so fast and chewing with my mouth open, but the Notorious D.O.G. hasn't really eaten since Thursday night. Before scared stomach took over and made me nauseous just thinking about it. After I shove the last spoonful of rice into my mouth, I slump back in my chair, thinking about how good it feels to eat hot food, cooked in a real kitchen.

Some people don't even have one house to eat in,

and this week I ate at two. Sunny has almost the same thing on every time I see him, but I have all these new clothes to change into after I cover myself in puke. And even though today was the first time strangers heard me rhyme, my parents and brothers are always here to listen to me. Everyone should have a place to eat and sleep. Everyone should have clean clothes. Everyone should get a chance to be heard and have people to clap for them. People should know Sunny's name.

WHEN SUNNY SINGS A SONG
EVERYBODY LISTENS.
THE SHOW HE BE GIVIN'
DON'T NOBODY WANNA MISS IT.

HE'S ALWAYS IN IT,
SHINING EVERY MINUTE.
A STAR WITH HIS VOICE,
 FROM THE START TO THE FINISH.

WHEN HE'S IN HIS SPOT
YOU CAN TELL THAT HE'S HOT.
FROM THE BOTTOM TO THE TOP,
HE GIVES EVERYTHING HE'S GOT!

We don't notice that Diego the cat is chilling under the dinner table waiting for scraps to fall until C.J. lets out a burp so loud that Diego runs, scared, out of the kitchen.

"Wow, look at that! It looks like you're magical, too, C.J.," Maria tells him. "Diego can make things I can't find magically appear, and your gassy breath can make *him* disappear. Amazing."

"*Beans, beans, the magical fruit. The more you eat, the more you toot,* Ri-Ri! This whole kitchen gon' be stankin' in about five minutes. And it ain't just gon' be me," C.J. sings, shooting the joke back at Maria, looking at our empty plates that were full of rice and beans just a few minutes ago. My stomach *does* kinda feel like something dangerous is gon' come shooting out any second, but not like yesterday's puke-fest. This time I just feel full and a little bit sleepy. But I have to do something first. As much as I want to hang out some more with my friends, it's time to go home. For once, I'm feeling like I know what to say. I gotta get home now so I can write it down for my presentation.

MONDAY

CHAPTER 18

MOMS TRIES TO ACT LIKE IT ISN'T STRANGE that she's walking with me to school for the second time in only a week, but at least she doesn't try to hug me or reach for a corny high five in public this time. She turns to face me at the bottom of the steps in front of the school and just pauses to look me up and down. I know Dad probably taught her how to dap me up, so it's kinda funny when she lifts her fist to bump mine just before I turn to walk into the building. There's no big breakfast leftover, wrapped up for me in my backpack, and nobody calling today *big*. It's just my second Monday as a fifth grader. I see Mr. James and run up behind him to tell him I won't be running out the classroom today.

"You promise not to leave us hanging this time?" he says, walking beside me toward the classroom door. As always, his shoes match his tie. This time the tie seems way too big, shiny and covered in polka dots. If it wasn't for those dots, I think he'd probably disappear into the wall of words a little bit, standing in front of us matching too much.

"I promise, Mr. James. I skipped breakfast and didn't eat too much last night, just in case." Just the thought of standing in front of the whole class again makes me feel a little *gurgle* deep in my stomach, but this time I feel sorta different. This time I feel like I really have something to say.

"Yo. Just remember that your mama don't like you wasting your food, bruh," C.J. says as he shuffles farther down the hall to Mrs. Leary's class. "If it gets real bad, just think about all those dishes she gon' have you doin' if she find out you covered the boys' bathroom floor in last night's dinner. We can't lose you to dishes, Notorious D.O.G.," he yells from the doorway before disappearing past Mrs. Leary's wrinkled, bony hand. I stand there for a second smiling like a goofy, hearing someone call me that in front of everybody. My hands tighten around the straps of my backpack as I walk into 5-B.

HERE I GO AGAIN, HERE I GO AGAIN!
I'M READY TO LET PEOPLE KNOW WHO I AM.
LAST TIME WAS WACK, BUT THIS TIME IS
    DIFFERENT,
HERE TO GIVE THE CLASSROOM A REASON TO
    LISTEN.

SUNNY TOLD ME TO LET MY VOICE BE HEARD,
SO I'MA DO MY THING WITH MY MOVES AND
    WORDS.
MOMS TOLD ME TO LET MY VOICE BE HEARD,
SO I'MA DO MY THING WITH MY MOVES AND
    WORDS.

I KNOW THAT I'M SMALL, BUT WHAT'S THAT
    MEAN?
CUZ WHEN I OPEN UP, THEY GON' HEAR BIG
    THINGS!

I AM SIMON BARNES, THE D.O.G.

AND LOOK, DON'T FORGET THE NOTORIOUS, SEE!

SUNNY TOLD ME TO LET MY VOICE BE HEARD,

SO I'MA DO MY THING WITH MY MOVES AND
    WORDS.

MOMS TOLD ME TO LET MY VOICE BE HEARD,

SO I'MA DO MY THING WITH MY MOVES AND
    WORDS.

☆ ☆ ☆

"Hey, Mr. James, ain't you scared he gon' run away again?"

"Like I said, Kenny, we all need a second chance sometimes. That was the whole point of Friday. To try things out. Now we all know a little bit of what it feels like to share our thoughts out loud in front of each other."

"Well, I ain't got all day!" Lil Kenny yells as if he's got a job and appointments waiting, making the whole class snicker at me under their breath. Maria stays facing the front of the class, careful not to turn around smiling too big at me. She knows how I feel about today.

"So we're all gon' be *respectful*, right? Cuz if it was us we'd want everybody to show us some respect when we're talking, too." I focus on the I KNOW I CAN that hangs over Mr. James's head, just now noticing how far below the words he's standing. Mr. James probably had the mark lowest to the ground on the wall at his mama's house, too. At first I thought he was so much taller than me, like everybody else, because of how much of his face his forehead takes up, but *nah*, Mr. James is a small guy, too. That big ol' corny smile he always got on his face makes it so I never noticed until now, though. Just like C.J. at the Halloween party dressed as his dad's favorite rapper, nobody messes with Mr. James, either.

For some reason, today Bobby's seated in the same row as Maria but across the aisle. Probably got into big trouble with Mr. James and now he can't sit in the back anymore. Just as I stand up to walk past him, a foot flings out from under his desk and I feel myself flying forward, my face almost eating dust. But Maria's hand catches the back of my shirt. Bobby mumbles something under his breath that I can't hear over Maria whispering, "It's okay, Simon. You got this, Notorious D.O.G." As Bobby's mumbles get louder, Mr. James walks around the side of the desks and sits in my seat. I've never seen a teacher sit at a kid's desk before, but for him it's easy. *People always come at us short people about being small, but I bet they WISH they could squeeze into just about anything,* I try to tell myself.

IT'S YO' TIME, SIMON, IT'S YO' TIME!
BETTER DO YO' THANG, BETTER GET YO' SHINE.
GOT A WHOLE LOTTA FANS OUT THERE JUST
    WAITIN'.
NEVER WORRY 'BOUT FOLKS OUT THERE HATIN'.

I WAS MADE FOR THIS, I'M A STAR AND I
    KNOW IT.
A FRESH YOUNG DUDE, NOW I'M FINNA GO
    SHOW IT.
AND EVERYBODY'S GONNA SAY, "HE'S THE MAN!"
REAL TALK! NO DOUBT! HOMIE, YES I AM!
WOOF! WOOF!

"Sunny Jackson is a musician who struggles with homelessness, and has lived in Creighton Park his whole life," I read from my first flash card. I look up from it for a second, seeing Bobby going back and forth between looking at me and glancing around at the class. He shuffles around in his seat for a little while, making the bottom of his chair screech across the floor, until Mr. James reaches from behind him, putting one hand on the back of his seat to hold it in place. "Until last week I never thought about where he lived exactly. Or anything else about him. All I knew was that he was the old man always sweeping up everybody's leaves and trash on my block.

"Then I found out he used to go to school here a long time ago, when he was a kid. And when he got older he started working here as a janitor cuz he never left. But before that, when he was a kid, he used to sing in the kids' choir at his mama's church, where he got to sing solos. Everybody clapped for him cuz he was really good. And when he wasn't at church or rehearsal on the weekends, he would hang out in Creighton Community Park. Back then it was different, so he used to be over there all the time, and he would get into all types of stuff. One time he even walked up on a girl who climbed a tree to save her cat. And when he got older he married her."

"Yo! Mista James, Simon up there tellin' love stories!"

"Relax, Kenny."

"Anyway, he used to be singing in these hallways when he cleaned Booker T., which was around way before any of us was even born. But then, one day, he lost his job because the principal said his job didn't matter no more."

"Dat's CRAZY! If we ain't have no janitors, the boys' bathroom would still be covered in your spaghetti chunks as we SPEAK!" Lil Kenny blurts out right before Victor G. slaps the back of his head and Mr. James gives him *the look*. "My bad." Suddenly I don't need my flash cards. Lil Kenny blurting things out and the way Bobby's looking at me make me remember something.

"Yeah, well. Sunny Jackson lost his job because the principal back then didn't think he was important, and a lot of people have been treating him like that ever since. He could sing so good that he started getting paid to sing for a while after he lost his job here, but that didn't last for long. He lost everything, and people started walking past him on the street and in the park, where he has to sleep almost every night, like he ain't even there.

"This past weekend I learned he's sixty-three years old, and if the homeless shelter down the street is too full he has to sleep in the park and find his dinner in the trash can if someone doesn't give him something to eat. He doesn't have somewhere to wash his clothes, and he doesn't get a lot of hugs because people think he stinks." *Moms is always trying to hug me.*

"But I ain't never heard anybody that sounds like Sunny. And he's one of the nicest, funniest people I know, who has all the best stories. He always remembers me and believes I'm great at things. He calls me his boy like he's my real grandpa. And he's always laughing and joking with everybody, even when he has a lot he could be sad about." For a little bit I don't know what else to say. I just stand there thinking about Sunny and the shelter and all of his friends and then I can't stop myself from laughing.

"Yo, what's so funny, Barnes? Gonna run out again like a little scaredy-cat?" Bobby's voice reminds me I'm still standing in front of the class. And it isn't the worst thing in the world.

"I was just thinking about how I almost saw Sunny's butt the other day. His pants are always too big and he don't never have no belt." Maria's hand flies over her mouth to control how much she wants to laugh. She remembers seeing that, too.

"I guess what I'm tryna say is that last week I didn't know nothin' about Sunny except that he was always nice to me and he was always cleaning up the sidewalks even though we never asked him to. I never thought about him at all, really. But now I know I should have known Sunny a long time ago. And there's a whole lot of people like him in Creighton Park who we should know, too. My dad and the people at the shelter taught me the people who live on the street are just like us. That they're people who deserve to be treated how *we* want

to be treated. We don't know nothin' about what happened in their life, and we shouldn't judge how they live."

Maria stands up at her desk and starts clapping like I just accepted an award. She claps so hard it looks like she's hurting her hands, but she just keeps smiling at me and keeps going until Lil Kenny's up to clap, too. He's probably just happy to have an excuse to make noise, but it still feels good. I walk back to my seat before I can mess anything up. I hope what I said was enough. Falling back into my seat as Mr. James claps on the way to the front, I hope Sunny would be proud of me. I'm glad the presentation's finally over, but when I think of the way he clapped for me on Saturday, I feel like there's more I need to do.

ONE MONTH LATER

CHAPTER 19

WHEN I GOT THE CONFIDENCE TO GO IN
front of the class to talk about Sunny, I wasn't
tryna make more work for everybody else. I wasn't
even tryna earn extra credit. But that's still sort of
what happened. Turns out Mr. James got so excited
about my presentation that he turned our oral presentations into even bigger projects where we had
to find ways to do something about whatever the
timely issue in our presentations was. I was cool
with that, though.

See, after school that day of my presentation,

when Moms got home, I told her all about what happened and she asked me what I was gonna do.

"About what?" I asked.

"So you learned *all* that about Sunny, and you not gonna do nothin' about it, son? Come on now, I know I raised you better than *that*," she said, staring at me over the kitchen counter while I worked on a different assignment. I scratched my head a little, feeling confused because I really didn't know for a second. All this time I thought I was just supposed to tell people about Sunny and then maybe something would change if more people knew.

Buzz, buzz. I jumped a little, not used to hearing the buzzer from downstairs ring. When Moms opened the door, it was C.J. and his mom standing there with bags.

"Sharon, Simon didn't tell me y'all were comin' by. Wassup, girl?" Moms asked, looking confused, as she hugged C.J.'s mom.

"Go on and tell her, Cornelius," Auntie Sharon said, looking down at C.J. as he shuffled back and forth with his plastic garbage bag.

"Clothes, Miss Barnes. I—I—I got some

clothes to give Simon." C.J. ain't never serious like that unless he's talking to adults. I didn't know why he was being so weird talking to Moms. I walked over to stand next to her at the front door and dap him up.

"Aw, baby, that's real sweet, but don't you think…they gon' be a little…too big for Simon?"

"They not for Simon, ma'am. They're for the kids that go to Booker T. who need them," C.J. explained, handing the bag to me. Auntie Sharon dropped her bag in front of me, too.

"Well, what am I supposed to do with this, man? I been done with my project."

"I don't know. Maybe you could give them to Mr. James. I told Ma about what you said in school and she made me clean out my whole closet, dude. Just take the bag. It's jerseys in there that I ain't wanna give away."

"That's an interesting idea, C.J. We were just talking about something like that, right, Si?"

"Uh…yeah…something like that." This whole conversation was making me sweaty because it sounded like more work, but Moms was kinda right.

What was the point in learning all that stuff about Sunny if everything was gonna stay the same?

The next day C.J., Maria, and I saw Mr. James walking around the cafeteria and Maria got him to sit with us. I told him about the clothes C.J. and his mom brought over to our house and something I'd started wondering: *Are there kids who go to our school who are like Sunny?* I knew I'd been smelling the weird smell in our classroom and I knew it wasn't something I was imagining. Mr. James just smiled and nodded.

"Yes, I've got a cabinet we can keep all those in. And washers and dryers sound amazing! And free lunch is already a thing. I like the way y'all think!" he said. "Let's talk about this some more this week." We were all surprised that talking about this felt so easy and that Mr. James was down. We're so used to adults talking about how doing things we wanna do costs too much money.

CHAPTER 20

SQUEEEAK. GOOSE BUMPS POP UP ALL over my body and I see the little hairs on my arms stand straight up like a bunch of soldiers. This is the third time C.J.'s gotten too close to the speaker while holding the mic cuz he won't just stand still. Dad stands next to him looking like he regrets letting us set up the first Creighton Park Community Outreach Open Mic. But it was my idea, and I didn't want to do it without my squad. Even though Miss Wanda won't let C.J. handle the mic by himself, she let him do the sound check. Now we're all suffering listening to him say *Mic check one, two, three* for the one hundredth time even though it sounds the same as it did the first five times. Dad yanks the mic from his hands and pushes it into the top of the mic stand, moving it farther away from the speaker so the squeak doesn't happen again.

"That's enough, kiddo. Go on over there and help Simon set up the chairs. You drivin' us all crazy. I think we got the sound covered," Dad says, nudging C.J. off the mini-stage we've built and out of the way. Somebody had to do it.

"Man, all y'all hatin'! Always tryna silence me!" I love my friend, but he be doin' too much sometimes. Even though Dad told him to come help me, he walks over and plops down on a chair near where I'm setting up and watches me work instead. At least he's far away from the stage and somewhere I can see him. I don't need him messing anything up on the first time they ever let anybody do this.

"Ain't nobody tryna silence you, C.J. Stop being so dramatic. Why don't you help make the signs?" Maria yells this across the dining hall so loud that C.J. can't even act like he didn't hear it. I give him a look and he drags his feet over, picking up a marker. With Moms working on her famous lasagna back in the dining hall kitchen and Dad making sure the stage is all set up, Miss Wanda has left the three of us in charge of chairs and signs while she sets up the decorations out in the front by the entrance so people in the neighborhood know today is special.

Just as I finish sliding the last few chairs into a row around the stage, I hear Maria let out a big ol' *EEEEP* from near the dining hall doorway.

"Mr. Jaaaaames! OH EM GEEEE!" I turn around to see Mr. James with a bag full of clothes in one hand and a box that says CREIGHTON CAKES in the other. He's got a corny smile stretching across his face like usual and high-fives Maria the minute he sets all his stuff down.

"It looks so cool in here, y'all. I like what y'all did with the place."

"Thanks, Mr. James! What's that?" Maria asks, pointing to the box, even though we all know what's in it already.

"You know, a little something to celebrate my

best students doing this cool thing in the community," he says, keeping one hand on top of the box so none of us open it before showtime.

"And me too!" yells C.J., walking over, staring at the box like he's got hearts in his eyes. "I'm helping, too!"

"You know all y'all are my students. Don't matter if you're in another class. I'm proud of y'all. So where should I put all this?"

"My mom's in the kitchen cooking. I think this box should go back there. We have a plastic bin in the corner over there behind the stage for stuff people want to give to kids at our school who need it. You can take the bag over there. Then you can sit wherever you want. People are gonna start coming soon." Mr. James daps me up before handing the cupcakes over to Maria to take to the back while he drops his bag behind the stage. I look across the room and can't help but smile at it. It doesn't look as sad in here as it did the first time Dad brought me. It almost looks as comforting as being at home. It makes me proud of what we've done in the past month. Before, I only thought of coming here as a homework assignment I was scared to do.

"All right now!" I hear Sunny's voice before I see him. He's the first person to walk into the dining hall, and he looks like a whole different person with his new haircut and wearing Dad's clothes. It's so weird how perfect Dad's old clothes fit Sunny. He walks over and squeezes my shoulder before walking to the front row of chairs to sit near Mr. James. He smells like the soap my dad uses, too.

"Simon, I need you, C.J., and Maria to help me start setting things out on the tables, okay? Everybody else is gon' be filling up these chairs any second now. We gotta move quick," Moms says, suddenly appearing next to me in her apron, looking a little sweaty. Her apron is covered in red sauce and she has a big tray in her hand. "I need help with all that over there." She uses her head to point at the other things sitting on the window ledge of the kitchen for us to grab behind her. "I know you don't think I'm about to trust you with this hot tray, do you? Not today, Si. Me and your dad got this. We have too many people to feed," she says, laughing to herself and walking away.

The room starts flooding with people from every corner of the dining hall. I didn't know this place had so many doors, but it's kind of cool to know everybody's gonna be sitting down together soon while we eat my mama's food and listen to people perform whatever they want on the mic. My eyes get big when I see some of the kids from my class walk in with their parents. Seeing them sit next to some of the friends I've made at the shelter is wild. I could stand here looking at this forever. C.J.'s booming voice snaps me out of it.

"Mic check, one two one two! We finna start! What you gon' do?!" Face-palm. C.J. and the mic strike again. Before Dad or Miss Wanda can get to him, he taps the mic a few times with his fingers and runs offstage and takes his seat next to Mr. James and waits all innocent-like for me and Maria to take our seats, too. Even though the front area is for me, because I'm the host and one of the open-micers, I made sure to have two seats saved next to me for my squad.

"All right, my boy. I think it's time. You got this. This is gonna be great!" Dad says quickly, squeezing my shoulder and walking over to stand next to Moms. I take a look behind the stage and notice the plastic bin is full. I look across the rows of chairs surrounding the stage and hear the crowd buzzing, everybody talking to each other. I look at the food tables off to one side of the room and see the steam floating up into the air from all the trays. My stomach grumbles. This time, not because I'm scared but because I'm hungry. And all this is kinda exciting, too. Miss Wanda's hand nudges my back softly.

"Go on, baby. Everybody's waiting on you."

From the stage, I see so many faces looking at me. In the front row my best friends in the whole world sit next to Mr. James, smiling hard. And not like the weird smiles Maria was giving me in class when everything felt so scary. They just look real happy. And so does everybody else. By the kitchen Moms stands next to Dad with her arms crossed over her chest, with Dad's arm sitting around her waist. Across from them, Markus crosses his eyes and sticks his tongue out at me, sitting in between Aaron and DeShawn, which makes me laugh. I take a deep breath the way Moms taught me and step up close to the mic.

"Hi, everybody."

Hello! Hey! Hiiii! I hear the crowd say back to me while I clear my throat and unfold my piece of paper.

"Welcome to the first-ever monthly Creighton Park Community Outreach Open Mic. My name is Simon Barnes. I go to Booker T. Washington Elementary School. And I'm gonna be your host. Tonight you're free to come up and share a song, a poem, a dance, or a rap, as long as it's respectful. This stage is for everybody who has something to share with the community. But it's…*especially*… for the people who come here every week. We have five open-mic performers who signed up at the front, and later on we're gonna eat. But before all that, we're gonna open up the show with some special guest performers. Starting with somebody many of you might know and love. Please give it up for my friend…Sunny."

Sunny stands up and steps onto the stage, patting my shoulder as I try to step away from the mic to get back down to my seat. But then he doesn't let me leave.

"Feel like rhymin' for me, Simon? Got something in that head of yours that you can rap...for me?"

 MIC CHECK, MIC CHECK, SUNNY AND SIMON,
I BET, I BET, Y'ALL GON' LIKE THIS RHYMIN'!
I DO THE RAPS THAT MAKE YA HANDS CLAP,
AND HE HITS THE NOTES THAT'LL MAKE Y'ALL FLOAT!

WHEN THEY PUT ME ON STAGE, I AM NOT
    GON' CHOKE,
CUZ I LEARNED LONG AGO, I AM NOT NO JOKE!
SO I GET MY HAT AND I GET MY COAT,
WHILE SUNNY'S SONG SAILS LIKE A BRAND--NEW
    BOAT.

THE D.O.G. CREW, MAKE IT DO WHAT IT DO,
GOT MY FAM ALL HERE, MR. JAMES IS, TOO!
NOW THE CROWD'S GETTIN' LOUD AS WE ROCK
    THE MIC,
BROUGHT THE WHOLE TOWN TOGETHER FOR
    SOME FUN TONIGHT!

WHEN SUNNY SINGS, HE BE LIKE, "MOVE YOUR
    FEET!"
WE GOT ERE'BODY DANCING TO THE SOUND OF
    THE BEAT!
I'MA DO MY THANG, THAT'S HOW IT'S GON' BE!
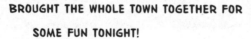CUZ I'M SIMON, THE NOTORIOUS D.O.G.
WOOF WOOF!

ACKNOWLEDGMENTS

Moms, you're the MVP and you've always been that to me. As kids, we used to hate when you'd take us to the library and we'd stay there for hours, but I guess it paid off, right? Your little boy has a book on shelves that real-life people can choose to buy. Praise Jesus! Would you ever have thought? I'm sure your answer is, "Uh, yeah—cuz you're *my* son." Well, here we are, and it only happened because of you. Thanks for being so gracious with me and loving me even when I didn't see what you saw. Now you can take your grandkids to the library or to the bookstore to check this one out! And you know what? I'll even see if I can get the author to sign it for them—just because I love you. Keep being a trooper. Love, Mookie.

Dionté, your love for reading has always inspired

me. The reason I started reading more is because I once saw you with a book that had hundreds of pages and knew I couldn't let you show me up. So, I went and got two books with hundreds of pages, and the rest is sibling-rivalry history! I'll let you think you're a better reader than me if you promise to take a look at this one in your spare time. Wait—never mind—you'll never be that, but you'll always be my big, little brother! I love you, dude.

DeJhari, you're the best sister I've ever had. To date, lovingly raising you along with Mommy has been one of my greatest accomplishments. I feel honored to be your brother, and to be honest, I think you're one of the biggest reasons why I love kids. I remember when you suggested that we start our own book club. It was such an awesome idea, and hearing you break down literature with such ease was absolutely beautiful. Your mind, your talent, your humor, your thoughtfulness, and your care for others are all tremendous things, and I can't wait to see how you continue to use who you are to help make the world a better place. I love you, Jhari.

Dear Nana and Papa, thank you for being awesome grandparents. Nana, you taught me how to read. 'Nuff said. Game changer. You win. But also, thanks for letting me take all those naps at your house, and for singing "In the Name of Jesus" to me. It was comforting. You have always been my comfort. You're definitely my #1 Nana. And Papa, thank you for helping me to T-H-I-N-K. You've always been so careful and thoughtful with everything, and thankfully, I think those traits have been passed down to me. Thank you for letting me grow up in the house you built. I love you both.

Elizabeth, you are such a G! I know you do this literary agent stuff for a bunch of people, but you've made me feel like I'm your only client. I don't feel like I'm just any random ol' author with you; I feel like THE author with you! You make this feeling happen. Thank you for taking a shot on a kid from Chicago who didn't know nothin' about nothin'. And thank you for always challenging me and fighting for me. You should be proud of your work, EB. Thank you.

Sam, from the moment we spoke together on

the phone that first time, I *knew* I was going to publish with you and Little, Brown. You believed in Simon, and I felt that energy from you immediately. In fact, I literally only chose LBYR because of you. You have been one of the most gracious and sweetest editors during this whole process, and I wish you nothing but success and happiness moving forward. Thank you, Sam.

Ellien, thank you for helping me bring Simon to life! God gives us dreams, but He also places people in our life who He knows will make those dreams come true. You're definitely one of those people for me. Thank you, friend.

Shout-out to all the kids on the West Side of Chicago. Y'all are some of the brightest, funniest, most beautiful people in the entire world. Don't ever let anybody tell you what you can't do. Put on for y'all's city, man. I love you to bits and pieces.

Dear Simoné, a full book couldn't completely capture what I feel for you. I have loved you since we were Simon's age, and I will love you until the last chapter of our life is complete. Thank you for being my everything, Monie. Love, Dwaynie Pooh.

Michael Hicks

DWAYNE REED is America's favorite rapping teacher. In 2016, the music video for his hit song, "Welcome to the 4th Grade," went viral, and it has since been viewed nearly two million times on YouTube. When he's not writing, rapping, or teaching amazing kids in Chicago, Dwayne can be found presenting at educator conferences across the US or loving on his beautiful wife, Simoné.